"A tour de force follow-up
to Maltese's A SLIP TO DIE FOR!"
— Chad Stuart, THE SIEGFRIED MATING

o o o

"Draqual is out of NYC but not out of mystery and
murder. A great second book in the series!"
— Bryant Tyler, SHAFT

o o o

*Other books in the STUD DRAQUAL MYSTERY series
by WILLIAM MALTESE:*

A SLIP TO DIE FOR

"An entertaining mix of camp and suspense, William Maltese's A
SLIP TO DIE FOR is giddy reading." — "Publishers Weekly"

"Left me panty!" — Adriana deBolt, VOYAGE OF THE TRIGON

"Murder and mystery masterly painted against a NYC backdrop."
— Anna Lambert, HOUSE OF THE BRAVE BULLS

"...the brilliant mystery persiflage tells of the ironic twists and turns
fate holds in stock for everyone once in a while." — kamu, SUD-
DEUTSCHE ZEITUNG (referring to the German-language edition).

o o o

Other books by WILLIAM MALTESE

CALIFORNIA CREAMIN' *An erotic short-story collection*

SUMMER SWEAT *An erotic short-story collection*

WHEN SUMMER COMES *An erotic novel*

o o o

What little breathing I managed became even more of a chore as billowing smoke grew thicker. I leaned exhausted against hot stone, part of a large seated Buddha that was mostly lost to the murk and the gloom. I turned head-on into a smoky breeze that reached me over a limestone Hari-Hara whose two left arms, one hand holding a seashell, laid broken at the figure's feet. I stumbled forward, past a terra-cotta deer whose folded legs gave it the collapsed appearance of a poor animal already succumbed to asphyxia.

Escape for me, if it existed, remained hidden within a river of smoke that grew thicker by the second. I surrendered to whatever my remaining survival instincts, held my breath, and plunged forward. Desperately, I tried to see through the smoke, through the soot, through the ash, and through the heat-distorted air. I hadn't a clue how long I could hold my breath, or how long I could keep going. My legs had about carried me to the limits of their and my endurance.

thai died

A STUD DRAQUAL MYSTERY

WILLIAM MALTESE

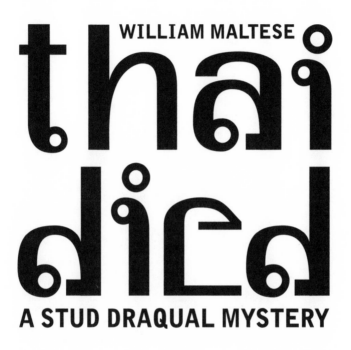

thai died

A STUD DRAQUAL MYSTERY

GREEN CANDY PRESS

Thai Died, A Stud Draqual Mystery *by* William Maltese
ISBN 1-931160-13-9

Published by Green Candy Press
www.greencandypress.com

Printed in Canada by Transcontinental Printing Inc.
Massively Distributed by P.G.W.

Whoever slit Rhee Dulouk's throat should never have let the victim, second mouth still bubbling blood, reach Jeff Billing. Billing would have been gone in another day ... or two ... or three. As he'd left the Philippines, Borneo, Bali. As he'd left Australia, Cambodia, Burma. As he'd left Spain, France, Germany.

For Billing, Thailand was just another stopover on the way to ... he never knew where ... just somewhere.

Rhee Dulouk wasn't a particularly great lay. He wasn't even Billing's type. He was just another wham-bam-thank-you-man some-one. One of many. A diversion. An exotic. Another notch on Billing's belt. One more fuck in Billing's ongoing fuck of the world. A keeper, beyond the first fuck, only because of a bit of pillow-talk that inter-ested Billing, who knew a little something about Far-East antiquities. But not likely to keep Billing's interest for long.

Therefore, Rhee Dulouk dead on someone else's doorstep would have been one thing. After all, there had been plenty of other bod-ies in Billing's life ... in the deserts of the Gulf, in the mountains of Iraq, in the back alleys of Afghanistan. Bodies left behind. Throwaways. Job-product.

Rhee Dulouk dead on Billing's doorstep, though... somehow... made the death personal. Not only to Billing but to me.

Though I sure as hell didn't know it at the time.

1

I'm used to being followed. That's been especially true since the New York City Slip to Die for murders. Then I was stalked by policemen, SEC agents, reporters, photographers, curiosity seekers, celebrity groupies, and the various human flotsam and jetsam found in the aftermath of any well-publicized crime.

Even before the Slip to Die for murders, though, I was often encircled by persons fascinated by a man prominent in ladies' lingerie. That category separate from the stalkers not only fascinated by my reputed sexual ambiguity but anxious to put better definition to it.

As a man who has had more than his share of being cruised by attractive gay guys (and by some ugly ones, too), I figured I had Jeff Billing pegged from first sighting. It had only taken a couple discreet inquiries to put his name to his admittedly handsome face and to his exquisitely hard body. Not to mention achieve confirmation of his sexual preference. Last, but not least, to receive word of his involvement in the recent death of Rhee Dulouk, young male Thai prostitute. He'd found the body bleeding out on his Bangkok doorway.

Therefore, I was confused at having so obviously misread all the assumed clues when I heard him shout at Roxanne Whyte, only minutes after I'd left her: "Whatever skeletons you've got buried, you can bet your sweet ass I'm going to get at them after what you've done!"

I'd spent years bitching and moaning about being cruised by every queer that ever was, only to feel ... feel what? ... because it turned out Billing had followed me only to get access to a woman. Whatever I felt, I was convinced it had more to do with me being duped into playing Judas Goat, and leading him to Roxanne, than it had to do with me being bypassed as a sex object. If it were ever assumed I'd aided and abetted him in any confrontation with Roxanne, I risked all kinds of complications in my life, personal and business.

Roxanne, who had made it as far as her limousine at the curb, was assisted by her well-muscled Swiss chauffeur, Nikolas, who ran excellent interference and soon had her locked inside.

At least Billing had done me the courtesy of confronting Roxanne after I'd left the immediate area. Thereby—hopefully—he'd left her entirely ignorant as to whom he'd followed to his prey.

Having already decided to make my way back to my hotel by foot, but interrupted by the outburst on the sidewalk behind me, I quickly made a further attempt to meld into the crowd. I needed only a few steps to become completely engulfed within a concealing maze of goods and services and the people who bought and sold them.

I sidestepped piles of exotic durians, jackfruits, and other succulent edibles. I threaded my way through a labyrinth of beggars, shopkeepers, ragged children, and well-dressed Thais. I hoped I blended in but, as an obvious American, I knew I didn't.

I was genuinely startled when brought to an abrupt halt by a hand exerting pressure to my left arm from behind.

"Hold up, handsome. It's time I gave you my official hello."

I was less than pleased to find it was Billing, and my expression must have relayed that. He immediately removed his grip, if not the sensation it created.

Standing there buffeted by the continuing swift flow of pedestrian traffic was as good a place as any to set Billing straight (if setting any gay "straight" were really possible). As an aesthetic who appreciated good looks and a good body, whether male or female, I refused to be won over by Billing's rugged attractiveness, even if it was enhanced by the faint pursing of his lips. A certain disconcerting something in his brown eyes reminded me of a once-favored polo pony who seemed uncertain as to why I'd whacked a riding crop so hard to its sweaty flank.

"Deny you've been following me to get to Roxanne Whyte, Billing!"

"Ah, you already know me! Then, why not call me Jeff?" He batted mink-colored eyelashes so thick and long more than one of my female models would have died for them; hell, I wouldn't have turned them down myself. "I'll call you Stud, right?"

"You'll call me Stud, wrong! Even Mr. Draqual borders on too informal."

I recommended walking.

Despite my none-too-subtle hint, he joined me in my zigzag within the unending mixture of people and goods for sale. I flashed him a sideways glance and compared his obviously well-conditioned handsomeness with New York Inspector O'Reilly's gone to pot look. The Inspector is someone I got to know because of the Slip

4

to Die for murders.

Why, these days, did I compare every man to O'Reilly?

John O'Reilly, in his early forties, is a man obviously ravaged by police work. His square jaw, cleft chin, and vertically carved left cheek, come together in a way that says (and says it loudly): One drink too many. Strike one! Two drinks too many. Strike two! Three drinks too many. You're out!

John O'Reilly is a man who has been on the edge too long, and he's too far into his free-fall to be pulled back to rescue. He has seen it all, done it all, been made deadly tired and jaded by it all. New York City is full to the brim with the likes of him.

And, yet, that afternoon, when he grabbed me from behind in that alleyway, mistakenly thinking I was out to spoil a police take-down, there had been a certain ... what? ... about the muscled hardness of his chest, his belly, his arms (yes, even his cock).

At the time, I'd felt thoroughly put-upon. What did I feel later? What did Dr. Melissa, my shrink, pull out of me ("Draqual, this is harder than pulling teeth!")? In a word: nothing. Because I didn't want to go there. I still don't.

In contrast to O'Reilly's more down-to-earth good looks, Jeff Billing's handsomeness fit right in with Bangkok's colors too vibrant; noises too loud; weather too hot; rain, when it came, too abundant; and food too spicy, too sweet, or too sour.

I was headed toward the distant Chao Phraya River where I hoped for quick transport to my hotel.

An unanticipated surge of oncoming foot traffic squeezed me off the narrow sidewalk. It was just my perverse luck to have Billing keep me from losing my balance and falling into the path of an oncoming tuk tuk.

"Thanks," I begrudgingly conceded. Granted, a tuk tuk isn't a two-ton truck, merely a three-wheeled tricycle that pulls passengers rickshaw-fashion through traffic-clogged streets, but .... I tried my best not to appear ungrateful but shrugged free.

"How about we decelerate to a slow trot?" he suggested. "Or, is one of us going to a fire?"

"I don't know about you, Billing..."

"Jeff," he insisted.

"I don't know about you, Billing," I persisted, "but I came to

Bangkok on very important business. Which I still have every hope
of successfully completing before I head home."

"All work and no play …," he said and left me to complete his
utter triteness. "Can't tell you how many times I've been tempted
just to come on over and say hello. I've got this gut feeling you and
I could really hit it off. How about we officially jump-start our off-
to-a-bad-start beginning with a friendly lunch? It'll be on me: the
least I can do for whatever trouble I may have caused you."

"'May' have caused me?" I stopped walking.

"You refer, I suppose, to potential problems with Roxanne
Whyte?" he divined. "I tried to wait until you'd disappeared down
the road, buddy, to put you completely out of the picture, but she was
just too fast getting to her car. Still, you may well be overreacting. I
can't imagine how she'd ever guess your unwitting part in all of this."

"Exactly what kind of skeletons do you think are buried in
Roxanne's closet?" I asked and immediately regretted my natural
nosiness. (Dr. Melissa—and do let me say a little about the good
doctor—would be cackling: "Told you so!").

Melissa J. (for Janling) DoLittle is a shrink. She's my shrink.
She's old enough to retire. She would like to retire. She will retire as
soon as she can wean those few of us fuck-ups she has left on her
roster. Whereafter, she'll comfortably nestle in among her expensive
gewgaws acquired from her few million billed-at-$250 an hour. Dr.
Melissa ("It's Dr. DoLittle, Draqual!") isn't one to sit back and not
ante-up her five-cents' worth as regards life in general, as regards
my life in specific.

She didn't want to take me on. She didn't want to take on anyone new. My father, who could be really persuasive when he
wanted, wanted her—for me (hell, I'm his only son!)—as soon as he
heard she was the best New York City had to offer. Daddy had two
advantages over any other poor schmuck out to reel in Dr. Melissa.
Dad was CEO of Draqual Fashions, haute couture silk ladies'
underwear; Dr. Melissa is a sucker for silk. Dad was the only
source, world-wide, of Draqualian silk… a very special silk, spun by
very special silkworms, who eat very special mulberry leaves, to
make very special cocoons pre-dyed, in Technicolor digestive tracts,
to very special perfection. I got Dr. Melissa; Dr. Melissa got a very
expensive Draqualian-silk teddy; I think nowadays she thinks she

got the shortest straw.

Jeff Billing's pregnant pause told me he wasn't about to explain any skeletons in Roxanne's closet.

"I'm not going to spread unsubstantiated rumors behind Miss Whyte's back," he said finally and sounded insulted I'd ever assumed he might.

I almost laughed in his face. "Well, excuse me! But you were hardly being discreet a few minutes ago."

"I can't be responsible for eavesdroppers."

"Eavesdroppers? For Christ's sake! I was nearly a block away at the time."

"Okay, I got a bit carried away. All I wanted was a meet. I've tried to set one up with her for ages."

"Are you researching some kind of book, Billing?" The last thing I needed, after the Slip to Die for murders, was another author in my life.

"Christ no!"

"Just what is it that you do for a living?" I was about to add, "... besides find bodies on your doorstep?", but I bit my tongue.

"Things." How vague could he get?

"I, too, have things to do to make my income happen," I said. "I can't do those things nearly as well by alienating one of my chief silk suppliers. So, if you'll excuse me ... as interesting as all of this might be."

My business with Roxanne Whyte, waiting somewhere in the wings, was only one of the things that made me see Jeff Billing as persona non grata. Another was his reputed ties, however tenuous, to the recent murder. I'd had enough of murders and the people who committed them.

"Hey, stud Stud, it's not as if I arrived in Bangkok with any advance notion of enlisting your help in getting me to Roxanne," Billing argued. "You and I at the same hotel, I merely heard you were seeing her regularly, on personal- and business-related matters, and I decided to take advantage to track her down. She's an extremely hard lady to run to ground if you don't have access to the good graces of her social secretary."

Whyte Silk Consortium was founded by Roxanne's late uncle. Everyone in the silk business knows of the key role Powell Whyte played in revitalizing the Thai silk industry after World War II. While the company isn't the only wholesale outlet for silk in Thailand, it provides the irrefutable guarantees of workmanship and quality that I, and my customers, expect and demand. I have my own silk-producing facilities in the States, but all of that output is very special, very expensive silk. It's never enough, especially not with my proposed expansion into men's ties.

"It's always been my belief that the rich people of the world, possibly you included," Jeff continued, "exist according to self-made rules and regulations that have nothing whatsoever to do with the laws of the land. I'm continually appalled by how some people can get away with literal murder ..." (a reference to the recent homicide?) "... while friends and relatives rally round to keep the skeletons from tumbling pell-mell out of guilt-littered closets. When people start pointing fingers and screaming about me being a no-good sonofabitch out to blacken a good name, there's usually a cover-up."

"Roxanne Whyte is a genuinely nice person," I said as someone who had come to consider her a friend as well as a business associate.

Whatever business Billing had with Roxanne, or thought he had with her, the less I knew about it the better.

"Well," he interrupted my train of thought, "shall we share the Chao Phraya Express, a water taxi, car taxi, tuk tuk, mini-bus, public bus, or do we walk the distance to our hotel?"

At least, I'd diverted him from any notion of a shared lunch.

I proceeded southwest on Ratchawong Road, Billing in tow. The chocolate-brown Chao Phraya River was straight ahead.

The Ratchawong Pier was right there, too, from which the Chao Phraya Express provided regular service every ten to twenty minutes. Suddenly, though, the Chao Phraya Express seemed entirely too commodius. I wanted a water taxi small enough to accommodate just a helmsman and me, Billing removed from the transportation equation.

I detoured around the pier and headed for the river.

I performed the prerequisite ritual of arm-waving, shouting, and sign language to hail a boat I figured to be just the right size. However, of the three boats that raced toward shore in response, it was a sizable dugout, with a low-power outboard, that took the lead.

"It looks a little small," I lied, as the boat came nearer. "Maybe you'd prefer waving down something for yourself that'll prove a little less cramped for the both of us?"

"It's plenty big," he said and winked.

The dugout captain was stripped to his waist and wore a pair of pants so spotlessly white they could blind from a distance. He angled his winning boat for a landing.

"Yes?" he called and maneuvered to where I could conveniently board without getting a foot wet. "Americans?"

"Right!" Billing confirmed.

The boatman was younger than I'd originally thought. Or, maybe he was older than he looked, which was more likely in a country where old people could look like teenagers. Whoever found a way to bottle their secret would make a fortune. If and when Draqual Fashions ever makes the giant leap into cosmetics ...

The Thai captain steadied his boat while I came aboard. Billing closely followed my suddenly-feeling-very-vulnerable behind.

The wake from a passing launch caused our water taxi to rock precariously on the resulting swells. Wood splintered only a few short inches from my left hand. Reflexively—in that I was far more familiar with bullets, these days—I dropped off the seat into the shallow well of the boat. The dugout went into a genuinely raucous dance upon the waves.

Our skipper went overboard. Billing came down on top of me, sandwiching me between him and the boat bottom. Gasping with surprise and the impact of his muscled weight, I inhaled a combination of dead fish, fetid water, and Billing's citrusy cologne. My face smashed damp and spongy wood.

There was a dull thud, like distant thunder.

I could no longer see where the bullet (had there been a second?) scarred rotten wood. Additional bullets might yet penetrate lower down and enter my warm and yielding flesh. A hole might yet be opened in the boat below the water line. The latter could be worse than a quick and merciful death by firing squad, in that the river is a notorious catch-all for sewage and pollutants. Germs and horrible parasites thrive in it. Neither Jeff (our present closeness made me suddenly think of him in the more intimate first-person), nor I, were likely to be possessed of the immunities enjoyed by the locals.

"Are you okay?" Jeff asked. His voice was low and surprisingly controlled. His heartbeat was at least two beats slower than mine.

"It's my arm," I said.

"You're shot?" he asked with obvious concern. His mouth was close to my ear. His breath was warm and lemony against my cheek.

"It's falling asleep."

"I hope it's not the boring company," he said.

At least he didn't laugh.

Breathing deeply, I tried to keep calm by reminding myself that we weren't dead yet. I wasn't so sure about the boatman.

"Who's shooting?" I asked. Would Jeff tell me if he knew?

"I'd love the answer to that one," he said with just the vagueness I expected.

One thing I knew was that I hadn't done anything lately to make anyone mad enough to gun me down. Fellow participants in the Slip to Die for murders were either dead or jailed.

The boat rocked in another set of waves caused by a passing larger boat. That other peoples' lives proceeded normally all around us was hard for me to fathom.

"You stay here and keep down." He shifted his weight atop me.

"Where are you going? Are you crazy?" I made an unsuccessful grab for him, my fingers grazing one very solid and firm buttock.

The sun, no longer blocked by his body, exploded its brightness on my eyes.

Hunkering back down, I cradled my head on one arm and tried to work the needle-pricks out of the other. I couldn't believe I was in a coffin-small boat, floating up and down, back and forth, as if in isolation from the rest of the world. Water sloshed against my container and against the shoreline, but the rotten wood of the boat muted the sounds. The loudest thing in my universe was my own galloping heartbeat.

I looked at my Piaget wristwatch. It had stopped, its gem-face shattered.

The boat tilted dangerously sideways and began to swamp.

I played rat, deserted the premises, landed in three feet of water that didn't stop my forward momentum, and was quickly out of the dirty river.

I heard only the drum roll of my runaway pulse. The world was a blur, a kaleidoscope of color. Unable to focus, I abruptly hit Jeff face-to-face with a force of a wrecking ball whacking a steel-fortified building.

Exposure to fear (as it always does), had given me a hard-on. It didn't take genius IQ to realize Jeff—yes, by God!—had one, too. Our collision of boners, and the sensations resulting, wasn't anything to which I want (nor do I want Dr. Melissa) to give any additional thought.

I turned away from Jeff and back toward the river.

A bedraggled and waterlogged Thai boatman made a last-ditch effort to board his outboard. It was his efforts to get back in, not a sinking ship, which had sent me on my merry way. In the end, he gave up his efforts and staggered toward shore. His pants were no longer pristine white but graveyard brown and water-weighed so far down his pretty much flat-ass-and-no-hips torso that I hadn't a clue what kept them from falling.

Miraculously, Jeff had a Thai policeman with him, who was saying, in English: "We'll need the boat as evidence." At the moment, the boat in question drifted, unoccupied, down river. "I'll radio from the car and have someone intercept it."

No doubt about it, I was pleased about police involvement as the officer jogged toward his squad car. What I said was a less complimentary, "Better late than never!"

A few minutes later, the policeman was back. Several of his cohorts dispersed a growing crowd of curious onlookers.

"You'll be more comfortable at the station," the cop told me and, then, took us there.

Jeff and the boatman were ushered down one hallway, I down another.

The man to whom I was turned over looked nothing like his assumed U.S. counterpart, Inspector O'Reilly, NYPD. This Thai policeman was olive-complexioned, delicately boned, almost pretty, with comic-book black-almost-blue hair, finely defined eyebrows, thick eyelashes, black eyes, cherubim mouth. He couldn't have stood more than five-seven in his impeccably tailored black uniform and his dazzlingly shined boots.

I didn't recognize his uniform, although that wasn't surprising. The Thai Police Force, a national organization, has all sorts of divisions and districts; I'm only intimately familiar with a few: Metropolitan Police, Provincial Police, Metropolitan Traffic, Highway Police, off the top of my head. It was the brown-uniformed Tourist Police who dealt with tourist-related crime, anything from credit fraud to too-high bar tabs.

I didn't recognize his uniform insignias, either, including whatever their designations of his rank.

"Lt. Col. Chuab," he said and filled in just one of the blanks. He extended his hand. He had a firm grip and a precisely brisk and short-lived handshake. "And, you're Mr. Draqual."

I wasn't surprised he knew my name, since I'd given it to one of the policemen en route.

"You're with the Samphan Thawong District Police?" I said. Actually, I wasn't sure if the scene of the shooting officially was in Samphan Thawong or in Chinatown, and I counted upon him to better pinpoint the geography and jurisdiction.

"Partly," he hedged. Which pinpointed nothing.

He motioned me into a chair on the visitors' end of a highly polished desk completely devoid of office paperwork, and/or supplies, except for a phone. He sat facing me across a mirror-wood surface.

"Partly?" I said in probative echo.

"My unit is mainly liaison. When something occurs which may overlap areas of influence, I'm called in by the Chief of Police to facilitate."

"And the shooting at the river overlaps just what, and how?"

"Well, for one, it's the second incident in which Mr. Billing has been recently involved. The first, as you may have heard, was the death of a male prostitute in Patpong, Gangrak District Police."

"You've insinuated a 'for two'."

"You keep high-profile company, Mr. Draqual," he said. "Roxanne Whyte, as well as her nemesis." As if he talked Sherlock Holmes and Dr. Moriarty; Dr. Jekyll and Mr. Hyde. "Investigations involving high-profile people often bring from the woodwork vested interests of all kinds, from all sorts, to muddy the waters. Just think of me as a 'spreader of oil' to calm potentially storm-tossed seas."

"My meeting with Billing was purely by chance," I said, in that I suddenly thought it important I get that point across clearly.

"And it was your first meeting?"

Although Jeff had been hovering for ages, "Yes, it was our first meeting."

"Initiated by ...?"

"Billing."

"To what end?"

"To apologize for his having followed me to Roxanne."

"Why did he need to get to Roxanne?"

"You might ask him. He's around here somewhere, I believe."

He smiled, friendly. He could smile all he wanted. I'm used to dealing with Dr. Melissa who is better at this sort of thing than he ever will be.

"You're aware of Billing's part in the homicide I've already mentioned." It wasn't a question.

"I'm aware of nothing beyond the hearsay that he discovered the body."

"And, of course, he had a sexual relationship with Rhee Dulouk prior to that young male prostitute's cut-throat murder."

"Has Billing been officially charged?"

"No."

My expression was, "Well, there you have it!"

What I said was, "And now you somehow connect Billing's relationship with the dead Rhee Dulouk, and Billing's discovery of the young male prostitute's body, with his attempted murder on the banks of the Chao Phraya River?"

Lt. Col. Chuab provided me with another friendly, albeit indulgent, smile. I waited for Mr. Bad Cop to come in and relieve Mr. Good Cop.

"Rhee Dulouk also regularly had sex with one of the guards at the new Powell Whyte Memorial Museum. The guard has since turned up missing."

I got far more insightful and interesting information than I gave.

"You might want to do Roxanne Whyte and yourself a favor

and steer clear of Mr. Billing in the future, Mr. Draqual. I do see where a man who boasts a military background in black ops, a discharge under honorable but less than clearly defined circumstances, a history of mercenary gun-for-hire activities, involvement—or non-involvement—in a recent Thai male prostitute's homicide, and, now, a shooting, might exude a kind of moth-to-fire attraction, but do remember the fate of the moth."

"As one moth to another, do you mind telling me why you haven't just expelled him from the country as an undesirable?"

"In a word, 'politics'. His father's admitted wealth comes into play. Wealth derived from his deep involvement in Los Angeles real-estate. Plus his father's considerable world-wide political connections. On a more local level, not everyone in Thailand dotes on Powell Whyte's memory. There are highly placed and quite influential dissenters who look upon Powell Whyte as just another Ugly American who was out to line his own pockets, any advantage to Thailand purely coincidental."

There was a phone call. Chuab's expression (as inscrutable as he tried to make it) told me something was up.

On cue, the door opened and a decidedly neat and attractive young policeman (made only less neat and less attractive when held to the ideal presented by his boss) handed over a thick file folder ("Thank you, lieutenant.") and left as quickly as he appeared.

I waited. (One of Dr. Melissa's favorite ploys). My expression was, "I'm curious but patient." (I only hoped it worked better for me than it does for Dr. Melissa, with me).

"We have a 'who' as regards your unfortunate incident on the river. Now, if we only knew Madam Elephant's interest in seeing Billing and/or you dead."

Which told me we had no major breakthroughs. "Madam Elephant" was merely the latest in a long line of frequently changing scapegoat top bad-guy monikers—Mr. Water Buffalo, Madam Nun, Mr. Lama, Madam Tiger, come to mind—used, at one time or another, to blame someone, for something, minor or quite horrific, when no other person or persons, group or groups, thing or things, could be proved to blame. Think: Boogeyman.

The Lt. Col. tapped the folder. "One Nathan Nakham was the shooter."

"My congratulations on your speed." It was doubtful O'Reilly and New York's finest could have been so swift.

"Our accolades are earned only insofar as we were able to back-track the bullet trajectory."

My expression was my best, "Please don't make me play twenty questions!"

"Nakham missed with his first shot. Conceivably, he then fired his second which overstressed and exploded his faulty weapon. Initial I.D. of him was made via his distinguishing body tattoos."

Which indicated that the Lt. Col. needed to await more positive I.D. for explanations far less nefarious than an illusive Madam Elephant siccing some gunman on Jeff Billing. More logical was how some white knight employee, or some loyal peon within the bowels of the extensive Whyte Empire, had taken it upon himself to rid Roxanne of the bothersome Billing.

"I would think an amateur would have been more likely to use faulty munitions than someone who killed as part of his everyday business," I said.

"Professionals, used to receiving the best weaponry, can grow as complacent and careless as anyone else," Chuab explained, conde-scendingly. "The weapon in question was part of a shipment hijacked out of Belgium three months ago. We know it was part of that shipment, because it, and two other similarly flawed rifles, were intentionally included as tracers should the shipment ever fall into unauthorized hands. Thai underworld figures have dealt in illicit weaponry for years. Our sources put Nakham in the employ of Kim Chang ten years ago, Rene Rawling five years ago, Bah Phumin as late as last year."

I looked at him quizzically.

"Mr. Mole, Madam Monkey, Mr. Tiger."

Which required a mug book or a bestiary?

"All of the above were involved not only in gun-running but in prostitution. Both of which, in case you didn't know, remain illegal in Thailand."

Go tell that to all the gun-toting whores. At least he'd managed to incorporate Rhee Dulouk squarely into his equation.

"And, Madam Elephant is ...?"

The police do occasionally put names to the monikers.

Invariably, though, they do so only after the body turns up.

Predictably, the Lt. Col. said, "The most recent changeover of criminal power was particularly difficult for us to follow. Variables, as always, included the complications of family ties, blood, friendships, alliances-of-convenience, and political connections."

To believe the police, it had been complications of family ties, blood, friendships, alliances-of-convenience, and political connections that had, a few years back, put a figurehead seven-year-old boy (Tan Ping: Mr. Rosebud), atop the underworld pyramid. Police identification, however, came only after the kid's mutilated body was fished from the Gulf of Thailand.

By pure deduction, we could expect to learn the true identity of Madam Elephant only after another shift in power fatally dethroned (and probably disemboweled) her. It was unlikely, then or now, she'd answer any questions as to why she wanted Jeff Billing dead.

It always seems incongruous that this fabled top underworld slot finds any takers, when its every reincarnation proves so precarious and so short-lived. Then again, the chance, no matter how tenuous, for power, and for the possibility of great riches, makes people do strange things.

"I suppose Lt. Col. Chuab told you what the cops think?" Jeff said. He climbed after me into the back of the squad car assigned to return us to our hotel.

I sank into a seat I wished was more comfortable. A dull ache pulled at both ends of my spine.

"Lt. Col. Chuab says the illusive Madam Elephant has you on her shit list," I said. "Any idea why?"

"Whoever the gunman was, I still suspect Roxanne Whyte is behind the shooting."

I leaned more toward a variation on that theme. "If not for Powell Whyte hand-carrying samples of Thai silk to potential U.S.

and European buyers at the end of World War II, a presently very lucrative industry would likely not exist. Thailand, and a helluva lot of Thais, would be a lot poorer today without what the Whytes did for the country's economy. Not to mention Roxanne's involvement in other facets of Thai industry. You start screwing around with someone responsible for employing a large segment of the Thai work force, and you'll make enemies among the rank and file as well as at the top."

Jeff closed his eyes.

Another look at him convinced me he hadn't been treated nearly as politely by the police as I'd been.

"Were they pretty rough on you back there?" All sorts of uncomfortable images rose to mind, although Lt. Col. Chuab had seemed downright civilized.

Jeff opened his eyes. He turned his head in my direction. He smiled. "You mean, did they pull out the thumbscrews, rubber hoses, and electric cattle prods?" He leaned forward and addressed our chauffeur-cum-policeman. "Did you use those on me, 'Jeeves'?" When he got no response, he settled back and turned another smile in my direction. It was a nice smile that showed nice teeth. "Nah! They were actually quite 'British' about it. Although, they did make it perfectly clear they disapproved of me being in Bangkok and doing whatever I'm doing. They inferred their disproval had something to do with the Whyte family having been quite generous to the people of Thailand. Being as chummy with Roxanne as you are, I suppose you know her uncle left the country the bulk of his extensive collection of Thai antiquities, most of which are still in Los Angeles, supposedly scheduled for shipment to Thailand."

"Actually, the first shipment has already arrived at the museum," I spoke with boastful authority on the subject.

"Ah, yes, the museum. One very important prerequisite set down by Powell Whyte in his will: 'The people of Thailand must construct and maintain the Powell Whyte Memorial Museum to house said collection.' A museum to be built and operated, from the trust Whyte laid aside for those purposes, with stringent security arrangements to protect the treasures. For if the museum isn't built, and/or adequate security isn't provided, the trust is dissolved, its

17

monies and—very importantly—the collection—to revert to ..." He locked his gaze with mine. "To whom do you suppose everything reverts, stud Stud?"

"Call me 'stud Stud' one more time and see what happens. As for your question, Roxanne inherited everything but the collection, and the funds set aside to take care of it."

"Give the very handsome man a Kewpie doll. If the Thais foul up, Roxanne gets the whole ball of wax." He sounded as if he'd made a very important point. If he had, I hadn't followed it. The museum was already built. The first part of the Powell Whyte Collection was already installed. A small party for museum bureaucrats and a few of their friends was scheduled for that very evening; I was counted among the latter.

Jeff shut his eyes again, and conversation ebbed. I thought he'd fallen asleep. If he had, our arrival at the intersection of New Road and Si-Phya foretold his nap would be a short one.

"In any of your recent conversations with Roxanne, has she mentioned any problems at the museum?" Jeff mumbled sleepily. However tired he was, I intuitively sensed something far more weighty asked than he made it seem.

"What kind of problems?"

"Oh, I don't know." It sounded as if he waged a battle between his desire to talk and his need to sleep, the latter about to win. "Maybe she mentioned a crack in the foundation, a rain gutter that doesn't work, or a misplaced figure of a bodhisattva, pre-Ankor style?"

"A misplaced what?"

"Apparently, none of the above," he responded wearily, "or you're very good at this acting-surprised stuff."

"Who said a bodhisattva was misplaced?" Had it been mentioned by Jeff's now-dead prostitute lover? Had it been mentioned by Rhee Dulouk's now-missing museum-guard john?

I'd been at the museum during part of the uncrating of artifacts. I recalled at least three of the deities worshipped in Mahayana Buddhism as enlightened ones (who compassionately refrained from entering nirvana in order to save others). Pre-Ankor style, though, didn't ring any bells.

"I refer to rumors, only rumors," Jeff said and tried to shrug it all off. "One can never place much faith in rumors ... especially when received during pillow talk ... especially when passed on to me by someone out to impress me with small talk. Except there does seem to be a helluva lot of resistance to my attempts to check the rumors out. Why do you suppose Roxanne absolutely refuses all of my requests for access to the artifacts prior to the museum's official opening?"

"Maybe because the museum opens to everyone so soon," I suggested. "Whatever you want to check out, you can check out then."

"At least, the museum is presently 'scheduled' to open soon," Jeff said. I didn't miss his don't-believe-a-word-of-it emphasis.

"You don't think it'll come off?" What was he getting at?

"All I believe, at the moment, is that we're about at our hotel." The car turned right off New Road onto Oriental Lane. "Which brings me to one final subject. I assume that your Lt. Col. Chuab..." (As if the Lt. Col. personally belonged to me!) "... suggested you steer clear of me after today."

The car stopped at the street entrance to The Oriental Hotel, and Jeff turned to me.

"It's been very nice to know you, but I guess this is good-bye," he said and exited the car. "Which is a pity. I foresaw definite possibilities for the two of us. Ciao, stud Stud!"

The doorman in livery gave me his de rigueur welcoming nod and ceremoniously opened the door.

I paused, as I invariably did whenever I entered the impressive lobby via its nondescript street entrance. The hotel had been built in the 1870s when the only really convenient transportation was by water; therefore, it had been designed for access and viewing from its Chao Phraya side. Unless you arrived by river, you couldn't really appreciate how the hotel's older pediments and ornamental façade outshone its more modern 350-room River Wing addition.

I picked up my messages at the front desk. A note from Roxanne said she would see me at the museum that evening. She confirmed the time that she'd send a car. There was no mention of her confrontation with Jeff.

"You've someone waiting," the clerk said. He motioned toward a small suite of lobby furniture in an alcove off to one side.

I headed in that direction. I was curious what business a ten-year-old boy could possibly have with me. I was curious that the portfolio in the kid's lap was scarily reminiscent of those carried by pimps who hawked their flesh-pot wares, via look-at-this-beauty snapshots, on just about every Bangkok street corner.

4

More scary was how, close up, the kid wasn't a kid at all and hadn't been one for quite some time. He was merely made up to look that way and had, from a distance, fooled even me. His school uniform was a dark-blue blazer, dark-blue shorts, starched white shirt, dark-blue tie, dark-blue knee socks, black shoes. His hair was cut so it straight-line banged all of the way to his eyebrows. His doe-like eyes had to be chemically dilated.

He sat on his section of the sofa like a little boy, his feet off the floor. A more comfortable position would have had him seated with his feet all of the way down.

"You're waiting to see me?"

"Mr. Draqual?"

He didn't stand but offered his hand. Which I took and found limp as a wet noodle.

As someone who continually works with models who put makeup on and take it off, I know it when I see it. There was definitely mascara on his eyelashes; maybe, there was even mascara on his brows. Definitely, he wore a bit of black eyeliner. There was a bit of blush along both of his cheekbones. Obviously, he'd used something to make his full lips their ripe pink. Seen close up, he had more than a couple of wrinkles, at the corners of his eyes and mouth, but they were camouflaged (expertly, I might add) by foundation and a bit of powder.

Thailand's active prostitute population, sometimes estimated as high as two million, was thought to be at least one-fifth male. Youth, and/or the illusion of youth, was always at a premium.

I was surprised he had been allowed in by hotel management. On the other hand, he was there to see me, and I was in Bangkok to see Roxanne Whyte. The Whyte name had tremendous cachet even at The Oriental.

"I'm truly afraid you're wasting your time." I had to give the guy moxy for having come right on in and staked claim to his isolated bit of lobby. "I've very little free time, this trip. Business. Business. Business."

He blinked his mascara-enhanced eyelashes. He smiled his pink-enhanced lips. He cocked his head slightly, as if doing so made him see me more clearly.

"Actually, I'm here in the hope you can help me locate my dear Nana."

He flipped open his portfolio to retrieve the top photo in a pile of photos. Beneath the one chosen was one of a completely naked young Thai with a boner the size of which forever belied the stereotypical Asian as small-peckered.

I was almost too absorbed with the neglected photograph and my amazed, "Good God, can that thing of his be real?", to register my visitor's, "Here's a photo of my Nana and me, when I was just a baby." He referred to the selected snapshot he extended in my direction.

He noticed my not noticing (and noticing).

"Ram is very popular, especially with foreign customers," he said.

"Ram?" I sounded like a myna.

"I can also recommend another young man who comes with even larger equipment, but ..."

"I don't believe I got your name," I interrupted. I took the innocuous family snapshot, glad he took the hint and closed his portfolio over Ram's disconcerting ram.

"I am sorry. My name is Sammy Ped Mai." He fished in his jacket pocket for an embossed business card that said: SAMMY PED MAI: PURVEYOR. So, that was what they called it these days.

A coincidence—I thought not!—that "ped mai" in Thai means spicy? What's more, a good rule of thumb, in Thailand, or anywhere else, is to avoid like the plague anyone who calls himself Mr. Sammy or Mr. Jimmy.

"Your grandmother is missing, Mr. Sammy?"

"Just call me Sammy," said Sammy.

"And you somehow think I can help you, Sammy?" I shook my head in disbelief.

"Yes, please," he said and patted the spot next to him on the overstuffed sofa.

"I really don't think ..."

It was his turn to interrupt: "Pretty please."

No one—thank God!—seemed to be noticing the two of us.

"Please, please, please," Sammy emoted. A childish temper tantrum seemed inevitable.

I sat down. It would take me a quick second to set Sammy right. I didn't sit down next to him, though. I took the chair directly across from him.

When he leaned forward, I thought for sure our knees would bump.

"I truly believe your friend, Miss Whyte, has absconded with my Nana," he said. Absconded?

"What?" The scenario had become all the more ludicrous.

"I truly do believe so," he said. He crossed his heart.

"Roxanne has made off with your grandmother?" I thought, perhaps, he or I was a bit confused as to the definition of "absconded" or "Nana".

"Maybe, she has even perpetrated more dire consequences," he said. Perpetrated? Dire? Consequences?

I took a good look at the frail old lady in the photo. She had wispy white hair. She was seated on what I can only describe as a milking stool. She had a cane in one hand and a baby in the other. To be literal, the baby was cradled in her arm. The height of the cane kept her one arm raised at an ungainly angle.

"And, what would be Roxanne's motive?" I couldn't help myself. (Sorry, Dr. Melissa!). I was fascinated by how Sammy might think he could ever bring me around to his way of thinking.

"Environ ..." He paused. "What is that name for people in your country who hug trees?"

"Environmentalists."

"Granny was a tree-hugger," he said; I thought for sure he'd opt for the more multisyllable word. "She was born and raised in a particularly lovely patch of much-beloved first-growth timber. Nana and I spent many enjoyable hours there."

What, I wondered, would Nana think of Sammy now in Bangkok, portfolio in hand? What would she think of his business card?—SAMMY PED MAI: PURVEYOR.

"One of Miss Whyte's companies decided to log the area," Sammy said.

Powell Whyte had not only left his niece with his silk business but with extensive interests in logging, tin, antimony, tungsten, iron and gas (and those were only the ones I'd learned about in passing). Sammy shook his head, as if genuinely distraught. His bangs slid down his forehead like windshield wipers over glass.

"So long and so loud did Nana protest that Miss Whyte came running."

I nodded in indication that he should, by all means, go on.

"Shortly thereafter, Nana disappeared without a trace. Shortly after that, the big trees were encircled by a large electric fence. Armed men stood guard."

"Why?" I couldn't wait to hear his explanation for this one.

"Exactly!" he said and left whatever the explanation hanging. "You tell me."

"Nana hugs one of the trees, and they wait for her to let go?" Okay, it came out wise-ass. But, really!

"And why, a few months later, did the fence and the trees come down, the guards no longer anywhere to be seen?"

Sammy Ped Mai was an interesting diversion. But, on a day like that day, filled as it was with so many diversions, his story of a tree-hugging Nana, missing in action, wasn't holding its own.

I must have telegraphed my waning interest.

"Just ask her about my Nana, will you?" he said. His hand was on my knee for emphasis. His feet finally touched ground.

"I have your card." I got to my feet.

"I can make your efforts worthwhile," he said. He looked at the portfolio in his lap, and his fingers caressed its cover.

"Really, I've too much business for any recreation, this trip," I said. "Thanks anyway." I'd been propositioned enough times to know how to make a non-homophobic exit.

"I have women, too," he said. In proof, his portfolio opened to a lusciously naked woman whose hands provocatively parenthesized her shaved cunt.

My cock began to harden, but it always has a mind of its own.

Quite detached from the expansion of my cock in my pants, I

was more interested in what kind of dye could possibly have produced the vividly hot-pink of the sheets on which the woman was sprawled.

I headed for the elevator, without giving Sammy Ped Mai a backward glance.

After a much-needed shower, I glanced over the several menus left on the desk in my room, providing a preview of the eating possibilities in the hotel for that evening.

The Normandie Room, with its floor-to-ceiling, armored, heat-resistant windows, a view of the familiar Chao Phraya River, planned a meal originally served on 20 April 1894: celery soup, fish in red sauce, fried veal with capers, potatoes, green salad, Siamese curry, and baked custard.

I called room service and asked them to send up a chicken sandwich and a cold beer. It wasn't because I found the Normandie Room fare of no interest but because there was a buffet scheduled for the museum party in just a couple of hours.

The kitchen sent up Mr. Asuk with my order. He's a small-boned and slender man of indeterminate age, with straight short-cut black hair, black eyes, rosebud mouth. Several minor acne scars on Mr. Asuk's forehead and cheeks keep him from being downright pretty (lucky Mr. Asuk!).

He has been around since my very first visit to Bangkok, back when my father was alive and dragging me along, under protest, to soak up a bit of the silk business. I already knew Roxanne at the time, although our connection was tenuous and not yet business. She attended Westover while I was at Groton, and she had minions at the helm of the Thailand business since her uncle had died and left it to her.

I waited until Mr. Asuk had repositioned my sandwich, beer, and glass, from silver salver to tabletop. I waited for him to open the beer bottle, pour much of its pale-brown contents, achieve just the right amount of acceptable head. Then, as usual, I tipped him big-time, just because he has been around since my Bangkok Day One.

"Oh, Mr. Asuk?" I stopped him on his way out. I convinced myself it was spontaneous but, even then, I knew it wasn't.

"Mr. Draqual?" He waited patiently, turned back in my direction. He looked as if anything I'd ask of him, he could deliver. Since we were in Bangkok, that was probably the case.

"I talked with Mr. Jeff Billing earlier." I wanted to seem oh-so-nonchalant. I wanted to pretend it was no big deal, although the incident by the river was, no doubt, already grist for the hotel gossip mill. "Though he told me his room number, I can't seem to recall it."

Mr. Asuk's expression told me what? There was a definite indentation of the slight dimple just to the right of his mouth. His lips were slightly pursed. A very few lines suddenly (and not unattractively) etched the outer corner of each eye. So much for my attempt at surreptitiousness!

"Never mind, I'll just call the front desk."

"Two-twelve," he said. Then, as if I might have forgotten my question, he said, "Mr. Billing's room number."

"Thanks."

He didn't leave immediately, though. He provided even more trace of an all-knowing smile.

"What?" I said. I'd known him long enough so his reserved demeanor no longer held up nearly as well as it once had.

"There seems to be a plague of recent memory loss," he said, as if he played guru on the hill who proclaimed obscure profundities.

I didn't have a clue.

He enlightened me. "Mr. Billing asked for your 'just-forgotten' room number, not ten minutes ago."

"Oh?"

"I gave him your room number. Should I not have?"

"Of course, you should have." He had, after all, just obliged me with Jeff's room number.

Why did I blush? Why did I hope my tan would conceal it?

Mr. Asuk nodded. He left. He pulled the door shut behind him. I bypassed my sandwich and beer in favor of an ornately framed mirror.

My cheeks were flushed—noticeably so, to my chagrin. My expression was ... what? Guilty? Why in the hell would my expres-

sion be guilty? Why had I asked for Jeff's room number anyway?
More disconcerting, why had he asked for mine?

I distracted myself by wondering what time it was. My broken
wristwatch was discarded in the bathroom. I checked out the clock
in the bedroom. It was getting late.

I ate my sandwich. I drank my beer.

I dressed in a double-breasted suit of experimental grey Draqual-
silk. We'd only just coaxed a few of our silk worms into secreting
grey. Our worms, which produced vibrantly colored silks in my
father's time, and had just begun supplementing with pastel shades
when he died, were most resistant, and continue to be, about giving
us grey. I'd exercised my executive privilege and claimed for myself
what had originally been slated for a couple of negligees and matching camisoles. Some customers' loss, my gain, in that while Draqual
Fashions didn't do men's wear, I wore ample proof we were capable
of doing so if ever we decided to go in that direction. The grey was
a light enough shade to make it an unusual, even a daring choice (it
behooves a fashion designer to be noticed!), but not a fashion faux
pax, for formal dress in the tropics.

My tie was of the same grey silk, although I eschewed a pocket
handkerchief which I've never found a fashion favorite.

All modesty aside, I looked pretty good. Although, I've always
figured myself burdened with facial features too finely chiseled; eyes
too purple; lips too bee-stung, a physique nowhere bulky enough to
warrant the moniker my well-intentioned father saddled me with.

Would Mr. Asuk's kind of acne scars give my features as nice a
masculine edge as it gives his? Once, I'd seriously contemplated providing myself with the same kind of scar that makes even more
rugged the already crag-like features of the German master who
taught me fencing my frosh year in college.

I ran the tip of my index finger in a slight downward diagonal
across my right cheek.

All these years later, I still remember, in every detail, the slight
line of puckered and contrastingly pale skin of Dieter's scar.
Surprisingly, it wasn't a scar he got from fencing but from a fall off
a horse when he was eight. Were it mine (I already have a couple
equine-caused cicatrices, both on the lower part of my body), I
would likely lie: a fencing scar is far more exotic. Dieter, though,

was as honest and as straitlaced as they come.

Speaking of straitlaced: "I'm not gay," he told me, at my very first lesson.

I'm always surprised by how many men in my life have said as much, without my ever having expressed interest.

"I have nothing against it," he said. Which is the second most oft-repeated thing said to me.

"It's just not for me," he said. That's the final part of the three-part litany: drum-roll, please.

By way of follow-up (really quite typical among men who find it necessary to announce their heterosexuality), Dieter proceeded into a lasting routine of strutting his naked stuff regularly anytime we shared a shower room. As if he remained determined to entice me into making a proposition just so he could provide, once again, his I'm-not-gay-but proof that he was a genuinely likable and liberal live-and-let-live sort of guy.

My self-admitted fascination with the naked Dieter never ... ("Never?" I can just hear Dr. Melissa).

My self-admitted fascination with the naked Dieter—"God, I wish I had the guy's body!"—was never sexual but literal; in that I truly wanted to shed my skin entirely and don his more appealingly chiseled pectorals, his scalloped abdominals, his muscled butt, and, yes ... yes! ... his truly humongous pecker. I feel particularly deprived by having a penis slightly less in size than the Masters-and-Johnson-specified average.

The red mark my index finger left on my right cheek, reflected by that Bangkok mirror, began to fade.

I went down to the hotel lobby to wait for the car Roxanne was sending. Nikolas was already there.

All I needed, after recalled comparisons with Dieter, was a more close-up comparison with Roxanne's blond Swiss-Adonis chauffeur and bodyguard.

Nikolas is a genuinely superb physical specimen, although he's on the verge of being too much so to appear well-tailored even in his obviously well-tailored clothes.

His blond hair, although cut short, is slightly spiked in front and is so thick there's no sign of disconcertingly pink scalp. His eyes are pale-pale blue, without being icy: think cloudless sky at high noon. His nose isn't too big, isn't too small, but fits his face as if made for it and not stuck on in afterthought. His full lips are the palest of rare coral pink. I'd like, one day, to see those lips smile, but I don't hold my breath. Nikolas is one serious fellow whose, "I'm not gay, have nothing against it, but it's not my bag," doesn't need to be put into words.

We headed for the Powell Whyte Memorial Museum.

I spotted it in the distance, between buildings, long before we reached it.

It was once described to me as "Strickette" by a well-respected architect who saw the building plans before construction began. The way she said "Strickette" made it seem as if she was saying a helluva lot (which, as it turned out, she was).

I waited for her to continue, but she had, as far as she was concerned, pretty much said it all.

First chance, back at my office, I enlisted my invaluable assistant, Betty, to search out "Strickette" as an architectural reference.

In the end, I was smugly pleased that my architect acquaintance thought me sufficiently knowledgeable in her field to be familiar with Jacques Strickette, a paraplegic (due to a high-school gymnastics dismount which had landed him on his head and broken his neck), who was, in his seventies, on the fast track to establishing himself as the genius Stephen Hawking of architectural design.

Strickette's Suisse Bank of Hong Kong designs were being converted into a mortar-and-stone building at the time I became familiar with him, and those designs (and the finished architectural marvel) were about to garner every conceivable commercial-design honor and accolade. Though he has never been out of Missouri, he's renowned for his late-blooming ability to provide memorable, stunning, magnificent, and beautiful buildings that perfectly fit their exotic locations and exude the perfect essence of their surrounding cultures. No way you look at a Strickette building and not know where in the world it is. His Suisse Bank of Hong Kong is Hong Kong. His Balivar Hotel de Bali is Bali. His Winset Building in New York City is New York City. His Powell Whyte Memorial Museum in Bangkok is ...

Think Sidney Opera House. Substitute brown-to-chocolate multi-layer cantilever tiers, rooflines gilded gables, lintels, pediments, decorative kalae, ngao, for white sail-like construction. Think flock of birds taking flight from the leading edge of a large reflecting pool. Think gossamer, weightlessness, airy. Marvel in how most of it isn't wood at all but durable spirenaldyne direnthinal steel textured by a process called sylvium-lamination-veneering to look like wood. The museum is designed not to burn and not to succumb to monsoon winds or rains. The building is floated on Teflon lotus pads to withstand earthquakes.

The museum is quintessential Bangkok ... quintessential Thailand ... quintessential Strickette!

The graceful curve of the entrance driveway is parenthesized by two arms of sky-reflecting water (think St. Peter's Square without the colonnade).

Nikolas dropped me off at the base of the wide seven-step stairway that funnels upward between four pillars, two on one side, two on the other. The inner columns equal each other in height but are taller than their companions. Twin marble elephants stand guard, life-size, one to each side, narrowing the entrance even further.

The massive fake teak double door is cast tilniquollinium with bas-relief grid-depictions of tales from the *Ramakien*. Entrance that night, though, was through the smaller door incorporated within the lower right-hand corner of the double door.

My name was checked off the guest list.

Immediately, I spotted Roxanne.

Roxanne isn't overburdened with extraordinary good looks. Her eyes are certainly an extraordinary pale tea-brown, made unique by seeming fragments of sun-blackened souchong leaves having made it through the strainer, but they're set a tad too far apart. Her high cheekbones are extraordinary, but one is a tad higher than the other. Her nose is a tad off-center. Her lips are a tad too thin. Her short-cropped hair is a startlingly premature white. All of it comes together quite nicely (real beauty often lies, after all, in the imperfections), but not so nicely that anyone is ever likely to say, "Ah, a model!"; or, "Ah, an actress!" On the other hand, it's all perfectly supplemented by an obviously skilled hair stylist's power-cut that requires no more maintenance than an occasional run-through of fingers ... by a wardrobe of well-tailored but never over-the-top couture clothes (and accessories) that fit her tending-to-thinness statuesque five-foot-eleven to a tee ... to produce just the right combination to label Roxanne, as correctly as any of the museum wall plaques put definition to the artifacts they accompany, as a mover and shaker, a CEO of a multi-billion-dollar conglomerate, who can hold her own and then some in a game played mostly by boys. She talked to Denny Mullet. Mullet, by the way rhyming with sleigh. Which always reminded me (every time Denny corrected someone's pronunciation that put him in the fish family), of that British TV sitcom that featured snob Hyacinth Bucket insisting people call her Mrs. Bouquet.

I should have liked Denny if for no other reason than that he was one of the few men who didn't meet me and immediately think I was gay. Right from the outset he considered me competition for Roxanne. Everyone, including Roxanne knew whose name Denny was out to change to Mrs. Mullet. Locked into his family's always struggling import-export business he, like Hyacinth Bucket, aspired to upward mobility.

I didn't like him. Not from Day One. And not just because he was so obviously on the prowl for Roxanne. He was just too much the Alpha male, likely in stereotypical compensation for his small physical stature (five-feet-six, if raised slightly on his toes; maybe a hundred-ten pounds if sopping wet). So aggressive and determined (poor-poor loser), he once accused me of cheating at croquet. Croquet for Christ's sake! As if I'd needed to nudge my ball any closer to his before I whacked his in a roquet (rhymes with damned good play) to begin the running of hoops that gave my partner and me the game. In the end Denny apologized, but I suspect it was only because I'd been teamed with Roxanne all that afternoon.

I avoided talking to Denny, and possibly having to discuss the earlier Jeff "mess", by procuring a champagne flute from the tray of a passing waiter.

Leisurely, I strolled through those rooms where the artifacts for the show were on exhibit.

When I'd first seen the vast array of incoming shipping crates, I'd been amazed and impressed by the sheer volume of just this first shipment, the majority of the Powell Whyte collection still in the States or en route to Bangkok. At the same time, I'd been introduced to Dr. Langau Kan-buri and Dr. Tenesla Rangliti, the museum's two authorities on Thai antiquities. I looked for either man within the crowd.

I found Dr. Rangliti, champagne glass in hand, literally gone red-face in an animated conversation with a middle-age, decidedly plump and matronly woman whose expensive clothes and jewelry were little help in their valiant attempts to make her less plump and less matronly.

Dr. Rangliti looked genuinely tired and put-upon. His eyebrows had become permanently knit into deep vertical grooves over the bridge of his decidedly large nose. His large upper lip, already made to seem larger because of an oh-so-thin accompanying lower lip, was additionally swollen by the man's habit of constantly biting at it with his rabbity two front teeth.

"Mr. Draqual!" If ever I'd seen Atlas about to be relieved of his Earthly burden, Dr. Rangliti was he!

He shook my hand, his palm just as slick with sweat as I remembered. He introduced me to his wife.

"I just love your lingerie!" she said. She tried to look embarrassed. She failed. She tried to look coquettishly demur. She failed. "I mean, of course, your company's lingerie."

I smiled, as captivated close-up by the variegated orange color-flashes from her ear-wear as I'd been from a distance.

"And, I love your fire opal earrings," I went tit-for-tat. "They're designed by Tom Munsteiner, right?"

Mrs. Rangliti's resultant wide smile revealed way too many yellowing teeth.

"Why ..." That's all she got to say.

"Good God, no!" Dr. Rangliti interrupted. "Jewelry designed by Tom Munsteiner? You have us confused with your rich American friends."

That Dr. Rangliti knew who Tom Munsteiner was said volumes.

"My dear, would you mind horribly if I took Mr. Draqual off to one side?" Dr. Rangliti said. "There's a particular artifact I promised to show him ..." Was the man a mind reader!? "... and it'll only take a minute."

"Actually ..." began Mrs. Rangliti.

In that fast-fading-behind-me fragment of her sentence (Dr. Rangliti having taken my arm to ferry me across the floor), I recognized an obvious and vigorous protest. We ended up in front of a stone shivalinga whose phallic shape (and purpose) I doubted very much Dr. Rangliti had any intentions of explaining.

"Thank-you, thank-you," he said. "I don't know why she bothers to come to these things when all she can do is complain. She always seems to think it's my obligation to entertain her."

"Ironically, there is something I'd like you to show me." I couldn't have any better put him under obligation had I planned it. "I understand around here somewhere there are a couple of excellent examples of pre-Ankor style bodhisattvas."

He eyed me strangely. Or, he seemed to eye me strangely. Or, he had something in his eye.

"Actually, we do have two," he said. "They're just in the other room."

Which shot all to hell Jeff's assertion that one or more was missing (and why was I even bothering to check on it?). Unless Jeff meant two others which were already gone.

The duo to which Dr. Rangliti referred me were right where he said they would be.

"Aren't they superb!?" he said. "I can't tell you how lucky Thailand is to get back these and other invaluable parts of her heritage."

By "misplaced", maybe Jeff meant ...

"Any chance one or both of these could be fake?"

I got an intuitive red-warning when Dr. Rangliti didn't laugh at my question. He didn't call it ridiculous. He didn't wonder aloud and indignantly where in the hell I'd gotten such a silly notion. He didn't jump right in and proclaim, on his dear mother's grave (were the dear lady dead) that both statues were true-blue, one-hundred-percent, certified, authentic.

"You're an expert on pre-Ankor style artifacts?" That was what he said instead. His tone was very low (actually breathless), with just a trace of attending tremolo.

Yikes!

"Good God, no!" I could only hope that I was far more convincing than Dr. Rangliti when he denied that thirteen-thousand-U.S.-dollar fire opal jewelry hung from his wife's large earlobes. I did have the advantage of telling the God's-honest truth, but how many an innocent man is sent up the river for not being convincing? "I've just always wanted to ask that question, because I know so damned little."

"Ah!" said Dr. Rangliti.

"Experts are overseeing the collection every step of the way," I let him know I was in the loop.

"Yes," agreed Dr. Rangliti.

"Sorry if my little joke took you aback for a quick minute."

Out of the corner of my eye, I saw Roxanne headed in our direction.

"Joke?" Roxanne said as she joined us. "I could use a laugh about now; let's hear it."

"There was this insurance salesman who stopped at this farmer's house and took notice of this farmer's really beautiful daughter," I said.

"Mr. Draqual asked me if either of these two bodhisattvas, pre-Ankor style, could be fake," said Dr. Rangliti.

So much for my hope that he'd already forgotten the incident.

Roxanne laughed. Trouble is, she forgot I know her well enough to distinguish between her laugh of genuine amusement, her laugh of partial amusement, her laugh of very little amusement. This was a laugh I'd not heard her laugh before.

"Oh, Stud, when did you become an expert in pre-Ankor art?" She shook her head in genuine disbelief.

"Never," I willingly admitted. "I was trying to be funny."

"See, Doctor, he was trying to be funny."

"Look, a joke ... a joke ... 'twas merely a joke ..." I said, "indulged by someone who wondered if there really were people who could tell the difference."

"I can tell the difference," said Roxanne. "These babies are real." Was her comment better late than never? "Dr. Rangliti?"

"Genuinely real." Was his comment better really late than never? "Dr. Kan-buri?"

Suddenly, conveniently Dr. Kan-buri was on the scene. Had the only other on-site expert on Thai art noticed our trio gathered at the bodhisattvas, wondered about it ... and come running?

"Miss Whyte, Mr. Draqual, Dr. Rangliti," Dr. Kan-buri super-fluously took roll.

Dr. Kan-buri is six-feet-six. His nose, his neck, his torso, his hands, his legs, his feet, are long and slim. His lips are thin. His black hair worn in a pony-tail, hangs down his back almost to his waist.

"Any chance either or both of these bodhisattvas are fake?" Roxanne said.

"Of course not," said Dr. Kan-buri. "No chance whatsoever!"

Finally someone was willing to step right on up to the plate and make a no-pause commitment. However, I would have been more impressed if the doctor hadn't come to the game with his pupils more dilated-to-pie-plate-size than Sammy Ped Mai's had been.

6

The buffet was announced "open".

I can't imagine the Israelites making their Exodus from Egypt any faster and more completely than the crowd channeled through the doorway and to the food.

My initial observation of the hungry museum-party crowd was tempered by reminders that they were, after all, mainly bureaucrats, ignored most of the time, who wanted to enjoy fully one of the rare moments anyone paid them any mind. Damn few, I was sure, were able to boast the kind of incomes that provided Mrs. Rangliti her orange fire opal earrings. The more decorous crème de la crème society crowd, who attended so many parties like this one they always looked bored by the free fancy food and gratis drinks, had their party scheduled for a later date.

I found myself suddenly deserted, so I took the opportunity to head to my favorite spot. The Powell Whyte Room is an intimate diorama tucked within the otherwise wide expanses of artifact-filled space.

The whole bedroom/den is from Powell's Bangkok house: dismantled, transported, and re-assembled. The result is a homey arrangement of desk, chairs, books, wardrobe, bed ...

"My favorite spot, too," said Roxanne.

I hadn't heard her come in. She completed her silent glide into a position beside me. She was so close that our sides touched. She was so close that I was engulfed within the subtleness of her expensive ambergris-based perfume.

"Come on," she said and led me to the red cord that kept the viewing audience a safe distance from the displays.

She unhooked the cord and motioned me on through.

"Let's give them apoplexy while I still can," she said.

"Them?"

"The 'watchers'. The men at the monitors who watch and record everything that the many eyes in this place see."

I checked for security cameras and didn't see a one.

"Watching devices are far more sophisticated, these days, than bulky cameras mounted on the walls," Roxanne said and insisted, with a nod, I preceed her on through. "Cameras, some as small as the head of a pin, are incorporated into this architecture. Don't ask me just where. There are way too many to mention, even if I did know. I do guarantee, though, this spot is being monitored at this very moment. Someone wishes I wasn't who I am, wishes the collection were all in the building so I could—although probably very politely— be told to please keep my hands off Thailand national treasures."

She laughed. It was a quite genuine laugh, this time around.

"It's really quite strange imagining that Uncle Powell has become a bona-fide Thai national treasure, after he pilfered Thailand national treasures for so many years."

She fastened the cord behind us and led me deeper into the room. Two wing-back chairs flanked the small fireplace. We sat and faced one another.

"You must forgive Dr. Rangliti," she said. "He overreacted. He's under a good deal of stress these days."

"Paying his wife's jewelry bills, you mean?"

"Of course, you'd notice the fire opals, wouldn't you? You used some of Tom and Bernd Munsteiner's stuff in one of your shows ... last Fall, was it?"

"Last Spring."

"Mrs. Rangliti's father, I believe, left her the little nest egg that allows her to indulge the occasional extravagance."

Which made Dr. Rangliti a liar when he insinuated the gems were paste. Why hadn't he provided Roxanne's excuse, if it were the real one?

"Dr. Rangliti's stress results from how all of this ..." She gave an all-encompassing wave of her arm, "... could go up in a puff of smoke, all the blame on him, should a fake suddenly materialize on his watch."

I pretended sudden remembrance of the provisions of her uncle's will, should museum security have proved inadequate. "Ah, Dr. Rangliti feared I gave you a reason to whip the collection right out from under him."

"His fears are not very well thought-out, of course, in that he knows the bodhisattvas are genuine. He knows I know the bodhisattvas are genuine. I'm afraid he just doesn't have a sense of humor."

With the whole collection Roxanne's to gain if museum security proved faulty, why would she cover up the existence of fake bodhisattvas by saying they were genuine? Did she know a missing museum guard had slept with Jeff's murdered trick?

"I must remember to offer additional apologies to Dr. Rangliti," I said. After which, maybe I should ask him to explain the conflicting testimony that made his wife's expensive baubles fake, on the one hand, and potential heirlooms on the other?

A rather attractive young man dressed in a stylish d'Avenza suit and apparently finished at the trough, made a start at coming into the room. He spotted us and made a diplomatic retreat.

"Lt. Col. Chuab gave me a call earlier," Roxanne said.

"Jesus H. Christ, here it comes!" I thought. I was only surprised that the inevitable had taken so long.

"It seems a friend of yours insinuated to the police that I might be behind a recent shooting."

"Do let me emphasize," I assured her, "that if you refer to Jeff Billing, he's no friend. The extent of our relationship is that I shared the whiz of a passing bullet with him, and begrudgingly, condescended to share a water taxi and squad car as far as our hotel."

"No harm is done," Roxanne said. "I was here at the museum at the time of the shooting, taking care of a minor problem. Enough people were with me to give me an alibi to convince even Mr. Billing I couldn't have handed over a defective weapon to his shooter, at the same time."

"What was the problem that brought you here?" I asked. Was it fake bodhisattvas that would allow her reclamation of millions of dollars in Thai artwork?

"It was an inconvenient problem of plumbing that, for the sake of our party this evening, had to be taken care of quickly."

As if Roxanne would be the one called in to take a plunger to a clogged toilet.

"How about some good news?" she veered.

"I can always use good news."

"I've something special planned for tomorrow, so don't make other plans. I'll pick you up at eight A.M. sharp. We'll head north and have a picnic on the way. We'll mix pleasure with business."

"That sounds good." Anything sounded good that even vaguely insinuated Roxanne and I remained on-track, despite Jeff's interference.

She checked her wristwatch as if the time she'd allotted me was up.

"Is it true you've absconded with Sammy Ped Mai's Nana?" I asked. I couldn't help myself.

Her wristwatch was suddenly forgotten, and she looked up. She shook her head. It wasn't done to deny her having run away with granny, but, "Is that little pervert a piece of work or what?"

"He pitched his tent in the lobby of The Oriental and waylaid me on my way in."

"Sweet Almighty! I'll see the hotel staff gets hell for having let the little queer through the door."

I knew she didn't have anything against gays, per se. She has several gays, men and women, highly placed within her organization and cares only that they do their work. Despite Jeff's trouble-making Roxanne never once commented negatively upon his well-known sexuality. Which meant it was Sammy, personally, whom she loathed.

"Did he try to convince you he was one of the thousands sucked into his present life-style by pure poverty?" she asked. "Did he insinuate his parents sold him into prostitution to make ends meet? Did he hint that he'd been manipulated, used, and abused, by flesh peddlers? Did he pretend he'd been brought to his present state of affairs through no fault of his own? If so, he lied every time!"

"Oh?"

"All on his own, he did what he did to get where he is today. He took to prostitution like a duck takes to water. He heaped enough shame on his family, all good people, to send most of them to an early grave, and he didn't give a damn."

"How old is he, anyway?"

"Well you might ask. He looks twelve or thirteen, doesn't he? Did you know every morning someone comes in and shaves his whole body, except for his head? I'll bet if he missed a depilation day, he'd sprout enough stubble to be mistaken for a porcupine."

"Should I divine from all of this, you've not done bad things to granny?"

"Mrs. Trang is just fine, thank you very much."

"She's not been cut down with her favorite strand of old-growth trees?"

"Is that the rumor the little monster spreads?"

Watch out, Sammy Ped Mai!

More full-bellied guests appeared at the doorway, obviously unsure whether or not to come in. Roxanne got up. "I really must mingle," she said.

This time, I unfastened the red cord that let us back into the realm of ordinary museum visitors.

Several people took their cue and came in. One couple—pot-bellied older man, thin younger woman—made a bee-line in our direction.

"I'll probably be here late," Roxanne said. "I'll have Nikolas stand by outside for whenever you're ready to call it an evening."

o o o

I didn't beat Nikolas to the driveway.

"Mr. Draqual." He opened the car door.

"Just to the hotel, Nikolas." As if he'd take me anywhere else, since he'd need to get back to the museum for Roxanne.

I picked up my computer-card key at the front desk and picked up my messages.

I pushed the elevator button. When the elevator didn't immediately arrive, I decided to walk.

I made it as far as the second floor.

I paused on the landing. I knew what I contemplated, but it wasn't easy to put any kind of adequate spin on it. Of what possible value was it if Jeff heard how Dr. Rangliti and Roxanne had come off more than a little taken aback by my suggestion that the bodhisattvas might be fake? Whatever validation might still be insinuated as to the truth of Jeff's theory had been diluted by how quickly the drugged Dr. Kan-buri had proclaimed, without hesitation, that the statues weren't fakes.

Conceivably, Roxanne might be embroiled in some kind of conspiracy to get the collection back. Conceivably Dr. Rangliti might somehow be involved with her. But, was it really conceivable to put Dr. Kan-buri into the conspiracy as well?

I pushed through the fire door between the stairwell and the second-floor proper. The door shut slowly behind me and sealed with a dull vacuum-like thud.

I stepped farther into the hall and noted the number on the door of the room directly across from me. I used it for orientation, in comparison to the layout of my floor on a higher level. My mental computations put Jeff's door directly down the hallway to my left. I squinted and saw the door where the corridor dead-ended.

I wasn't committed, was I, until I knocked, until Jeff answered, until I was invited in, until I went in, until I told him ... ?

With a dull low-decimal whosh that still managed to make my ears ring and physically slid me backwards, Jeff's door came off its hinges and rushed down the hallway to meet me. The numbers on the door went dizzyingly from low line on an optometrist's eye chart to lead-line big "E".

7

While I didn't know where I was, I had obviously expended a good deal of time and effort to get there. I was very, very tired, and my entire body ached very, very much.

Darkness surrounded me. There wasn't a pinprick of light to hold out hope of any exit from whatever deep pit I was in. I groaned my exhaustion and my frustration and my pain. I tried to make sense of the senseless.

"Is this Sleeping Handsome who awaits my kiss to revive him?" I couldn't place the voice. I was in some Mad-Hatter's dream sequence. I pinched myself, which only added to my pain.

My eyes were shut. My battened-down lids resisted, as if heavily weighed with coagulating glue, my effort to open them. When I finally succeeded, the intrusion of light constricted my pupils and interfered with my ability to focus.

"Where in the hell am I?" Bed sheets dangled all around me, like drapery.

"Safe and sound at the hospital. The doctor says probably without any lingering after-effects. Oh, you can count upon some short-term ones, to be sure: dizziness, aches, pains, that sort of thing. On the whole, though, you're very lucky."

The voice came from a fuzzy blob that grew increasingly more defined around its edges.

Jeff Billing came to mind. I tried to sit up and actually succeeded with assistance. Only then did I realize I was in a bed that was hung-round with partitioning curtains.

"It seems you had the misfortune to walk the halls at the same time someone decided to blow my room and me to Kingdom-Come. Luckily for me, I had gone for a spur-of-the-moment walk to clear the cobwebs. Luckily for you, you were down the hall at the time. Were you coming for a visit? I would never have forgiven myself had you ended up dead, by proxy."

Roxanne chose that particular moment to sweep in. She stopped so fast, just inside the doorway, she probably left skid marks.

Her gaze, with accompanying indefinable expression, went warily but purposely from Jeff to me and back to him again.

They were like two dogs coming across one another, for not the first time, and made skittish by past experience. I expected either or both to begin marking territory. Walls and floor were saved from splashes of piss only by Jeff opting for a diplomatic retreat.

"I'll check in later," he said to me, nodding in Roxanne's general direction (neither friendly nor hostile), and skirting her on his way on out.

"Thank God, you're conscious." Roxanne's attention back on me, she sat in the one available chair, squinting quizzically. "How do you feel?"

"I feel woozy."

"I suppose, Mr. Billing wasn't too modest to brag about how he showed up on the scene and provided you with mouth-to-mouth that you probably didn't even need?"

"Come again?" Was she kidding? Wouldn't I have remembered something like Jeff's mouth pressed up close and personal against mine, his hot breath pushing air into my lungs?

"Do you deny the sparks arcing between the two of you?" she asked. "When I came through the door, I swear there was enough electricity bouncing off these walls to cause spontaneous combustion." She folded her arms in what Dr. Melissa would call a defensive posture.

God, but I'd grown tired of how thoroughly cock and cunt were the end-to-all-ends for so many people! How much time and effort I'd wasted in rut before I'd seen the light! If I hadn't seen this coming from Roxanne, it was because I expected far more from her.

Thank God for the distraction provided by the arrival of the small-boned Thai doctor whose thick glasses rode her nose like a fat man astraddle a flea. "Is this our supposedly comatose patient?"

"Stud," said Roxanne, "this is my dear friend, Dr. Philipa Changmai."

Dr. Changmai produced a small flashlight and examined my purple eyes with her deeply peering black ones. She asked me to stretch my arms and alternately touch my forefingers to my nose.

"What you need most is rest," she said. She had a pleasant singsong pronunciation of English.

"He is going to be all right?"

"Everything points toward that happy prognosis; yes, my friend," Dr. Changmai confirmed and wiped her brow with the back of her hand, as I was but one more patient in a very long work shift. "However, we must make sure to monitor his condition carefully for the next few days."

"Next few days!" I had no particular fondness for hospitals, and nothing, so far, made this one an exception.

"It's a good sign that he doesn't look forward to a hospital bed and hospital victuals," Dr. Changmai said.

"Tell your administrator that I want this adjoining bed reserved

41

for me," Roxanne said. "I'll be staying."

"That is your prerogative, of course," Dr. Changmai consented, "although your own bed will certainly be more comfortable. Mr. Draqual isn't likely to be up to much slumber-party talk or activity after the sedation I've prescribed for him."

"I'll stay," Roxanne insisted.

"I'll inform the staff, then, that we've a VIP on board," Dr. Changmai said, nodding politely as she left the room.

Miss Chou (said her name tag) was quickly arrived and departed, delivering the contents of one exceedingly large syringe to my bare left buttock which I inadvertently offered up to her through the gaping back flaps of my hospital gown.

"Very nice ass," Roxanne said; or maybe I was already hallucinating from the effects of the fast-acting sedative. "You just get some sleep, and I'll try not to take unfair advantage of you while you're unconscious."

Much later, still under the influence, I heard a door open.

I heard a whispered, "Miss Whyte?!" It was repeated.

Roxanne's—"What time is it?!"—guttural response came from the bed that adjoined mine.

"A break-in at the museum, Miss Whyte. That Billing guy has been shot."

I tried to come down from the clouds on which I was high-flying. Helplessly, I continued to drift ... drift ... drift ...

Jeff Billings was naked as a jay. His body was a study in anatomical perfection. His pectorals were square. His abdominals were scalloped. His arm and leg muscles were powerful supplements to his Praxiteles-sculptured torso. A thin veneer of fine brown hair fanned the top of his chest but concentrated, straight-line within the deep groove of his pectoral cleavage, for a vertical bisection of his chest and mid-section as far as his shallow innie navel. His thick, circumcised, and vividly pink-headed cock was stiffly erect. As he walked toward me, his cock rocked—back and forth—back and forth—like the up-jutting tine of a very large metronome.

It wasn't until he stood before me and put the tip of his forefinger against my nose for its slide downward over my lips and chin and along my neck to my chest, that I looked down and realized I was as naked as he was; my cock was laid out along my lower belly. Jeff's sliding finger stopped just short of touching the head of my dick.

"Jeff!?"

"No." Dr. Changmai said; and I opened my eyes. "Anyway, not last time I looked."

I blushed, although I was well aware that (thank-you, Dr. Melissa!) no dream, homoerotic or not, necessarily confirms lustful thoughts. Certainly, this dream hadn't confirmed lustful thoughts toward Jeff Billing! What it meant, though, I couldn't begin to fathom. I could only thank God that it hadn't progressed to embarrassingly wet status.

I wondered how my calling out Jeff's name had been misconstrued by Roxanne, last seen on the adjoining bed. "Roxanne?" The adjoining bed was empty.

"They do say the third time is a charm, do they not?" Dr. Changmai encouraged, and her smile grew wider.

"Dr. Changmai, it is, then," I obliged. I slid up in bed. I felt the worse for wear after my exit from my thoroughly disturbing narcotic-induced slumber.

"Bingo!" the doctor congratulated. "I began to wonder, there for awhile, about your memory, but all's well that ends well. And, since we speak of wellness, how well do you feel this morning?"

I searched for an adjective to describe my last memory of Roxanne in the room. Instead, I said, "Was there anything in the morning's news about a break-in at the Powell Whyte Museum?"

"No," Dr. Changmai replied. If she found my question strange, she apparently was prepared to humor me. "And I'm quite sure I would have noticed anything so extraordinary. We all so rejoice in the return of our treasures to their rightful homeland. A break-in would undeniably be newsworthy."

"How about the shooting of an American?" I hoped it was a dream.

"The shooting of an American, or of any foreigner, certainly would have made the news."

She unclipped her small flashlight from the neckline of her tunic and aimed its beam into my right eye.

"Maybe I did dream it?" I gave myself the benefit of the doubt.

"Ah, maybe you did!" She bobbed her head in ready agreement. "Most certainly, it was a dream. Such dreams are not uncommon in the aftermath of traumatic experience and an ensuing sedation. Fortunately, even the worst dreams are beneficial in sorting all the random thoughts that clutter the mind during consciousness. Do you know that people who don't dream go quite mad? So, you must be thankful for your dreams, whatever those dreams, and be assured that even nightmares become less so as the trauma that triggers them becomes less a part of your life."

"I'll try to keep that in mind."

"So, aside from the dreaming?"

I took a few seconds to isolate my aches and pains. "I've felt better but, considering everything, I guess I'm all right."

Dr. Changmai moved the light to my left eye then clicked it off and replaced it on her tunic.

"Your latest prognosis, doctor?"

"I really can't come up with any real reason to veto Roxanne's request to move you," she said, "if Roxanne agrees to bring you back for a checkup in a couple of days or so."

"Move me where?"

"Of course, you should feel free to stay here if you so prefer," Dr. Changmai offered. "Although if I were you, I'd be more inclined toward accommodations Roxanne might come up with."

She took my wrist to check my pulse.

I wondered about Jeff. He had to have known the security at the museum was tight and designed to thwart professionals, even ex-black-ops agents, from illegal access. Anything less than the best security would have compromised the handover of the complete collection to Thailand. Jeff couldn't have hoped to penetrate such a high-tech system. Had he really tried?

"You've spoken to Roxanne this morning?" I asked.

"Oh, yes," Dr. Changmai confirmed. "She called in and asked me to release you to her care. It's rather difficult to say no to such a generous patron. Luckily, I'm not asked to go against my better medical judgment on this one."

"You talked to her on the telephone?" I tried not to make it sound like the third-degree. "Do you know what time she left the hospital this morning?"

"No, but I suspect it was as soon as she was sure you slept soundly. Sleeping on one of these beds, without sedation, is not an easy thing to do."

She flashed me a smile.

"I can tell you when she's due back." Dr. Changmai glanced at her watch. "In approximately an hour. Which means I'd better get a nurse in here with your clothes if you're going to be ready." She headed for the door, stopped, turned back. "The clothes you wore when you checked in were, I'm afraid, a bit the worse for wear. Roxanne sent some clothes to hold you over until you have access to your own things from the hotel."

So much for the brief life and times of Draqual Fashions' first special-grey man's double-breasted suit!

She left, replaced within seconds by Miss Chou carrying a bag which turned out to contain a fresh pair of skimpy underpants, a pair of slacks, a shirt, and rope sandals. "Miss Whyte is a very nice lady," Miss Chou said in parting.

I was fully dressed when the phone rang.

"Well, aren't you, as of late, as prone to attract disaster as a magnet is prone to attract iron?" said a welcome and familiar voice that belonged to neither the expected Roxanne nor to Jeff. "Do you know you made the national news?"

Betty Meiken, quintessential Girl Friday, is my most invaluable asset at Draqual Fashions. Without her, especially before I'd been brought securely into the fold, the company my father founded, and I right along with it, would likely have ended up in the toilet.

"Actually, I do quite well, considering," I said.

"Want me to catch the next plane and hold your hand ... or hold whatever?" Though she and I have evolved into a hands-off relationship, there are many times we've both been tempted.

"And leave the company without its rudder?" I totally disregarded that as unacceptable. "I don't think so. Draqual Fashions can manage without me, but manage without you?—Never!"

"You certainly sound full of your usual line of you-know-what, but I'd appreciate it if you'd be a tad more careful. Is business still on track?"

"I meet with Roxanne again in a few minutes."

"See if you can wheedle some tie-dye silk from her, will you? Draqual tie-dyed Thai-silk ties: how's that for tongue-twister ad copy?"

"Your wish is my command."

"Then try harder to stay out of trouble. And try harder to keep in touch. Do you know how many calls I had to make to track you down? Your cell phone is what? Lost? Damaged?"

I hadn't a clue. A, B, or A and B.

"What time is it there?" I said.

I pictured her checking her watch.

Right on schedule, she said: "It's going on midnight."

"I promise I'll call you later," I said and rang off.

However, I didn't hang up. I thumbed the receiver, and got the operator. She told me all out-going long-distance calls had to be made from one of the hospital's international phones. I went to look for one.

I went through the time-consuming bother of a call ... a collect call ... from a foreign country ... where the operators (and I include those on the U.S.-end of the line, too), didn't seem to understand a word of English.

"Hello," finally—said a weary voice from the other end.

"Dr. Melissa?" I said, interrupted by the operator's query as to whether or not "that person" was prepared to accept a reverse-the-charges call from Bud Blackwell in Bangkok.

I could picture the good doctor, clear as day. She wore the same sexless flannel pajamas she always wore whenever I dropped in on her at some ungodly hour.

Although the doctor had at least three Draqualian-silk nighties that I personally knew of (one from my father, two from me—her access to Draqualian-silk had been the deciding factor that allowed me to join her stable of fuck-ups), I'd never yet seen her "in" silk.

"Bud Blackwell?" she said. It was as if the operator, a patient ("client" as Dr. Melissa called us), had told a falsehood that the doctor, if only given the time and patience, would cajole her to confess.

"Stud!" I loudly identified myself to the phone's mouthpiece. "Stud Draqual."

"Someone calling for ... Dr. Melissa?" Dr. Melissa said.

Oh-oh! She always insists I call her by her title and surname. When we have face-to-face sessions, she has little success in enforcing the rule. At a distance of a few thousand miles, though, all she need do was hang up.

"I'm calling for ... Dr. Doolittle-who-talks-to-the-animals," I said.

No way she would have liked that reference, either.

"Will you accept the call?" said the operator, who had to be convinced we weren't trying to gyp the phone company by speaking in code.

"Why not?"

Good girl! She knew how to butter me up. She knew how to make me see the advantages of providing her with another Draqualian-silk nightie. Maybe, I'd even give her one cheaper than at-cost. Maybe, I'd even give her one for free, so she'd have tangible proof of how she'd "been there" for me, during my "horrifyingly traumatic time in Bangkok".

"I'm having dreams," I said.

"You're allowed to have dreams," she said, "especially as our handsome-as-hell national newscaster reports you were 'lucky to have survived the explosion.' Speaking of handsome-as-hell national newsmen whatever do you suppose happened to Gerald Kaney?"

She knew damn well Gerald had ended up dead, in a red Draqualian-silk slip. I'd played amateur detective to help the police solve the murder.

"You have any sense of deja-vu, here, Draqual? The news says you've been shot at, and now this explosion..."

"I'm here to buy silk. Can I help it if shit happens?"

"Is your hotel room on the second floor of The Oriental?"

Insightful, clever, old bag!

"What does that have to do with the price of tea in China?"

"Did you really call just to blow smoke up my ass?"

"I had a dream about this guy. Really."

"Which guy?"

"The one whose room blew up."

"Did you dream this dream before or after this guy's room blew up?"

"Before."

"You were on your way to his room to tell him about this dream, when ..."

"No way I'd tell him about this dream. It was ... well ... you know ... ?"

"Of course, I know, since I'm a mind-reader." Her sarcasm dripped thick as honey.

I can't imagine anyone pays this woman for sympathy and gets his money's worth.

"No way I can tell you about it over the phone," I said. "It's 'that' kind of dream, if you know what I mean. Which, we both know can mean something entirely different ..."

"Which, we both know can mean you'd like to get this guy in bed and fuck him, or be fucked silly."

"Nice talk!"

"Whatever happened to you wanting to go to bed with Inspector O'Reilly?"

"Where do you come up with this shit?"

"Maybe it's time to take your analysis to a higher plain. I know you'd rather not, but ... oh, hell, why don't you just begin at the beginning?"

"Why didn't you have the professional insight and good sense to ask me that at the beginning?"

I hung up and figured to get great pleasure from any of her attempts to get reimbursed for the call. There were times that I wondered if the good doctor, up there in years (I'd looked her up in the appropriate volume of WHO'S WHO, and she was 72), had begun to lose her marbles. I liked her better in her younger (67-year-old) days when she was less confrontational; although she never was one to just sit back, nod, and let the patient talk out the clock.

"You want me to pay for that call?" I'd say. "You're the one who did all the talking."

Truth be told, I felt better after I hung up on her. Go figure! Probably, it was just having someone on the other end—anyone.

I heard my name being called over the hospital PA system.

Roxanne didn't look as if she'd been routed from bed in the wee hours of that morning to deal with a break-in and shooting. She wore a pale yellow skirt with matching jacket. There was a small spray of green baby's-breath-like flowers in her jacket-lapel buttonhole. Her cotton blouse, a cool pastel blue, had a button-down collar that enclosed the loop of her pale yellow silk tie. Her perfume, exotically complex, was something I wished I bottled under my own label.

"How do you feel, aside from the bad dreams and all?" she asked.

"Dr. Changmai told you about the dreams, did she?" Thank God, Changmai didn't know the half of them!

"She also told me such dreams are nothing to worry about. I agree." No mention, yet, that Jeff had broken into the museum and been shot. "Ready to go?"

"Go where exactly?" I'd welcome whatever the change of scenery.

Roxanne's eyes narrowed, and she grinned mischievously. "Four-nine-six Litchi Klong Road. You'll like it ." Before she said more, someone knocked. "Ah, Nikolas!"

I managed to get myself into the wheelchair without assistance. Nikolas supplied momentum. Roxanne walked beside me.

"Does the front desk have my forwarding address?" I asked Roxanne as I was whisked by. Billing just might try to check back, if he was still able.

"Whoever calls will hear you were well enough to leave." Which didn't answer my question.

If he wasn't dying of a bullet wound, where was Jeff?

Roxanne's limousine was parked right outside. I felt five times better once I was inside it, wheelchair and hospital left behind. I settled deeply into the rich smell of luxurious leather. It was good to be alive, especially in a world of exploding hotel doors and bullet-fire on the Chao Phraya River.

"You already look considerably improved away from the sick-room environment," Roxanne said.

Should I ask if I had dreamed her midnight summons?

I was still asking myself that question when we pulled through the gates of our destination.

Four-nine-six Litchi Klong Road was the home of Cecil and Atrea Simms.

"Off on their once-a-year holiday to visit the kids and grandkids in the States," Roxanne said.

She guided me through the main house to a table and chairs arranged within the shade of a garden tamarind tree out back. Nikolas disappeared and was replaced by three household servants—a cook, a maid, and a house boy.

"The house was vacant," Roxanne said, "and I said to myself: 'Self? Wouldn't this be far better for Stud than any hospital room?'

All it took was a quick phone call to make it happen."

The house and the garden, the latter ablaze with bougainvillea and flamboyants, surpassed even The Oriental Hotel as a setting conducive to convalescence.

"Cecil's father was in Thailand with Uncle Powell during World War II," Roxanne said. She had taken a chair opposite mine. "These days, he's into tin mining. He met Atrea in the Sixties when she came over with a roadshow to entertain the troops headed for 'Nam. She'd just won Miss Something-or-Other—Miss California, I think."

If Atrea was the attractive blonde in an evening gown holding the parasol in the picture on the grand piano, she could certainly have once been Miss Something-or-Other.

"Cecil's hobby is architecture," Roxanne continued. "Once you get your second wind, I think you'll be able to appreciate what he's done with this place."

"I certainly like what I've seen so far."

I've been in several Thai homes, and this one would appear to be traditional only to a novice. The rooms were connected by closed walkways, not by traditional open breezeways. The stairway was on the inside, not on the outside. The carved window frames faced inwards not outwards. A classic Thai structure would be entirely unpainted. While Cecil and Atrea had left the inside walls natural teak, the outside was coated with the dull-red creosote introduced from England during the last century. Other anomalies included a modern bathroom, greeted by me with ultimate joy and relief; lots of Italian marble veneering the entrance way; and a large Baccarat chandelier in the dining room.

"This place is a clever jigsaw of seven old houses that Cecil disassembled at Pak Hai and re-assembled here," Roxanne said. "Of course, he's incorporated a few unique touches. The carved partition between the drawing room and the master bedroom once graced the entry of a Bangkok pawn shop."

Did Cecil have anything to do with the dismantling and re-assembly of Powell Whyte's bedroom/den?

The home's extensive outside, devoted to trees and plants, was a noticeable extravagance in a city desperate for living space. Such free areas occur only in the compounds of the very rich, or of religious sects, or of corporations. The equally isolated gardens of The

Oriental Hotel conjure just the same images of earlier times wherein men and women indulged shamelessly in quadrilles, waltzes, polkas, lawn tennis and croquet, on well-manicured grounds.

"The klong's namesakes," Roxanne said and pointed to the row of evergreen trees that disguised the filthy and garbage-strewn canal that could just be glimpsed through breaks in the foliage. "There were thousands of *Nephelium Litchi* in Bangkok at one time, but not by the time Cecil bought the property. He had to import those from China."

The servants reappeared with a breakfast as untypical of Thailand as the house. There was no kao tom (boiled rice soup with pork, chicken, or shrimp), but freshly squeezed orange juice; ham-and-cheese-and-mushroom omelets; hot, buttered scones; hot chocolate with great dollops of decadent whipped cream; papayas, pineapple, pomelo, tangerines, and bananas, attractively arranged in a highly polished wood bowl.

I realized this was the day Roxanne had scheduled our picnic and a special surprise.

Regretful of our forced change of plans, I mentioned as much over a forkful of omelet. Roxanne removed the small spray of flowers from the lapel of her jacket. I accepted the one delicate stem she offered. It supported a minute run of minuscule green blossoms.

Roxanne identified the small flowers as expertly as she'd identified the trees along the klong. "*Goodera lipisin*. It's an unique orchid variety only found in a small patch of jungle outside Kumpu-wapi."

I wasn't surprised that I held an orchid whose multiple pinprick flowers were nothing like the large and fat-lipped, vagina-like blooms popular for senior proms. I'd had a college professor explain, more than once, that any family of flora can come in an infinite variety.

Roxanne unfolded one of the white linen napkins on the table. She took her remaining flowers and laid them in the center of the cloth. She folded the linen over the small bouquet and applied a pulverizing pressure with the heel of her hand. Unfolding the linen, she revealed a luminescent stain more full-bodied and gloriously green than the crushed flowers that had made it.

"Wonderful!" I exclaimed.

"Happy coincidence, this," Roxanne said. The clipped short nail of her index finger tapped the cloth with its resulting stain. "This botanical miracle was dropped into my lap, roundabout, by a little

51

old lady, up around Kumpu-wapi, whose main income source was a stipend from her dissolute grandson. She supplemented what he gave her by doing embroidery and lacework. She prided herself on this particular green, which none of her rivals in the village could figure out how to duplicate. It was granny's little secret. It provided granny's little nest egg. Its earning capacity, though, suddenly verged on extinction when the only patch of forest in which the orchids grew was suddenly rumored to be up for sale. Granny figured it was my company that was out to do the chopping. We'd done a lot of lumbering in her area; thus her mistake. Actually, we'd checked the timber in question and rejected submitting a bid on it. The trees were mostly soft woods, and not enough of them to warrant the bother and expense of logging. It was more a project for some mom-and-pop operation.

"She could have taken her complaint to the people of my lumber company. What do they know but lumber? The offices were too far away, though. As I said, we'd picked up and moved to greener pastures. However, since the lumber company was mine, and the silk company was mine, and the silk company had facilities close-by, she went there. She wanted them to see that the trees remained. She claimed she was a local citizen concerned with the environment, that too much timber was being cut down everywhere. She insisted that cutting down this stand, too, was a big mistake. Sooner or later, the world would not have enough trees to provide oxygen for any of us to live. Up until then, she'd made no mention of little green orchids. She never really wanted us to know about them, any more than she wanted any of the old ladies in her village to know. Except, what do the people at the silk factory know but silk? They told her they were sorry about the trees, but if she wanted to talk to anyone about saving trees she should go to people who knew a little something about trees."

Roxanne laughed and shook her head.

"At which point, granny got hysterical. She accused us of trying to ruin her livelihood. She wanted to know how she was going to live on just the meager allowance from her mentally unstable grandson. All granny had to buy her any little extras was the revenue from her lacework and embroidery. All that made her lacework and embroidery stand out from the rest was her green thread. When the trees came down, what would happen to the green orchids that grew among them? What would granny do when there was no more green dye to set her work apart?"

"You do live under a lucky star," I said. I tried to think of the last time a windfall of such magnitude had dropped in my lap.

"Even then," she said and repeated it for emphasis, "what if she'd been talking to someone who wouldn't have known the existing potential if it jumped up and bit him on the ass? Believe me, I have plenty of just such people working for me. As luck would have it, though, she talked to Mr. Sabop's nephew."

I knew Mr. Sabop. He was head of the Whyte Silk dye works. I liked him.

"The nephew thought it was a pretty green. He thought his uncle might find it of interest."

"He liked it. You liked it," I divined. "I like it."

"We bought the land after all. I had the precious few orchids transplanted to a controlled greenhouse environment. Whyte Silk Consortium has since come up with this." She produced a square of Thai silk from an inside pocket of her jacket. The green of the material was of an even deeper and more luxurious hue than that of the linen, as well as excitingly different from the more famous Draqualian shade naturally secreted by the very special silkworm population I house in my New York State production facilities.

As an expert on silk, I knew the exceptional when I saw it. I took the square from Roxanne and, fingering it, was totally impressed by how the silk's natural sensuousness was enhanced by its radiant color-shifts within the green spectrum.

"It took awhile," said Roxanne, "to isolate the botanical chemicals and synthetically duplicate them. But we finally did it, even improved upon it, if I do say so myself. We have a few minor problems to work out before we can produce any kind of volume, but we've managed one fifty-yard bolt of silk. Granted, that's not much, compared to what we hope to make available in the very near future, but the bolt is yours if you want it."

I had an epiphany: "We're talking Sammy Ped Mai's grandmother, aren't we?"

"We fattened Mrs. Trang's savings by quite a little, by way of a finder's fee," Roxanne said. "She no sooner had cash in hand than her no-account grandson showed up and demanded his cut. He gave her a nasty black eye. When my people found out about it and told me, I immediately had her relocated to somewhere Sammy can't get to her." That answered that question. However, I was far more interested in the answer to quite another question.

"Did you have any dye at all left over for a few yards of tie-dyed silk?"

"You are interested, then?"

My obvious enthusiasm had already blown any real chance I had to bargain successfully. "Can Draqual Fashions afford it?"

"Consider it yours," she said, "as well as whatever yardage of tie-dyed we can manage. We can probably even get you in at the production facility to catch the tie dyeing in progress."

Some designers avoid the technical aspects of cloth production. It's only the final result that matters to them. I'm not one of them—not anymore, anyway. It might have to do with my involvement in my own silk production. It certainly has to do with my evolution from my earlier years of not giving a damn to my present state: I consider anything I can learn about a particular bit of yardage a help in translating it into a Draqual original. My successes, especially with silks, prove I do something right. "When?"

"As soon as we're sure you're up to it," Roxanne said. "Which shouldn't be long at all if you don't overdo it in the next twenty-four hours."

She excused herself, promising to return that evening for dinner.

Her way of walking, especially as seen from the rear, is definitely sexy. Not the distant, unattached, cool sexiness of a fashion model's exaggerated look-at-me, look-at-my-clothes sashay down a runway, but something far more subtle. The difference between ice and ice cream.

I was adjusting my boner to a more comfortable alignment within my pants in the aftermath of Roxanne's exit, when the house boy arrived with a phone.

"Draqual?" The voice on the other end of the line wasn't one I recognized. "Stud Draqual?" As if he mistook me for—my mother? If I don't make a concentrated effort to lower my voice over the phone, people not familiar with the cruel joke telephone communications play on my vocal cords can be confused and think they're talking to a woman.

"Yes," I said, in my butchest, low-level dulcimer tones.

"You're a difficult man to track down." There was no mistaking his guttural for other than masculine. "I had to call in a couple of markers to ferret your number from the private files of one Dr. Changmai."

Which told me what about the prospects that Jeff Billing would ever check in, even if he wanted to?

"And you are?"

"Why don't you call me Kenneth Critzer?"

Why don't I "call" him Kenneth Critzer? As opposed to calling him what?

"Well, call-you-Kenneth Critzer, what can I do for you?"

"It's what I can do for you."

"Okay."

"I've something to sell you that may very well improve your health. It can even extend your life-line, especially when you take into consideration your recent tendency to find yourself in harm's way."

"Want to get to the point?"

"Want to know who is out to kill you and Mr. Billing?"

Kill me? I laughed: Ha-ha! No one wanted to kill me. I was merely an in-the-wrong-place-at-the-wrong-time, innocent bystander.

"You mean, you know who wants to kill Jeff Billing, don't you? In which case, you might want to contact him."

If Jeff (bullet-ridden?) was in any condition to accept incoming calls.

"If you keep yourself rutted in that mind-set, you'll likely be gone by morning," said Mr. Critzer.

The last part of his sentence was somewhat obscured by static.

"You've bugged the goddamn phone?" He repeated the sentence, only this time, he made it a statement.

A distinctive click punctuated our connection. Another click was followed by the dial tone.

In every movie, it's the stereotypical warning that the good guy's phone is bugged. Of course, this wasn't a movie. My caller's accusation was stuff and nonsense. Obviously, he was mistaken about my life being in danger (other than via association with the apparently doomed Jeff).

Nevertheless, I unscrewed the phone mouthpiece.

"Don't get carried away," I told myself. "You're seeing spooks where none exist. Your mind is probably still scrambled from the explosion."

The telephone innards, lifted from their plastic mold, revealed an independent dime-size disk.

I'd never seen a listening device, except in the movies, but I knew one when I saw one. Its presence injected a whole new unwelcome dimension to recent events.

Was it only two days ago I'd assumed my life had returned to normal after the upset of Slip to Die for murders? When had things gotten out of control this time? How deeply was I into this, whatever it was? Why had Roxanne, seemingly on the spur of the moment, brought me to a house with a bugged phone?

Was Roxanne merely harmlessly curious as to what Jeff might say to me regarding his aim to muddy her reputation?

I removed the offending device and put the phone back together again. I felt out of my depth, not for the first time in my life.

Like a kid throwing a tantrum, I spontaneously flung the bug through the shrubbery of Litchi trees. With smug satisfaction, I heard it ricochet off a tree, then heard it provide a small, muted plunk as it hit the water. Of course I should have held onto it for evidence. What would I say to Roxanne when she offered an oh-so-innocent, "Bug? What bug?"

I was about to make a futile attempt to recover the device from the muddy klong, when the phone rang.

Hesitantly, I picked up the receiver.

"Stud? Jeff here."

Was I pleased to hear his voice? Was I angry? Was I relieved? Was I fearful? Was I beset by all of those conflicting emotions and more?

"I suppose you heard that Roxanne had me shot at the museum."

So, it hadn't been a dream, then.

"Actually, she was at the hospital when she found out," I came to her defense.

"It's called having deniability, good buddy. Happens in the military all of the time, but it doesn't take, for a second, the real blame off the decision-making generals, even if they do get away in the end."

"Where are you?"

"Do you want to come visit? I'd like that. Actually, that's why I called. I've managed a couple of interesting museum photos, for all my trouble. Even you might be persuaded of their significance. How about I call you later to set something up? I don't want to talk too long, because your phone might be bugged."

"Actually, this phone isn't bugged." I could speak with authority.

"Well, just to be safe." He figured I didn't have a clue!

"It's not bugged, because I just de-bugged it."

"No kidding!" His tone implied the unlikelihood of any male designer of women's undies (and soon, men's ties) having the proper know-how to disable spying technology. "Well then, are you up and about?"

"I can take a few steps but don't ask me to dance."

"A few steps are all that are necessary," he assured me. "Just take them at three o'clock this afternoon, down toward the Litchi trees. I'll have a boat waiting to take you across the klong. With luck, you'll be over before anyone can follow."

"Follow?"

"Come on, guy! My recent misadventure very likely turned up on some museum surveillance camera. I've momentarily managed to stay out of sight, but it doesn't take a genius to know they'll be prepared to use any and all means to try and find me. That'll include bugging your phone and watching you like a hawk."

The phone went dead, but there weren't two clicks this time: just the one, and the finality of the dial tone that followed.

However did I get into these predicaments? I was in Bangkok to buy silk, for Christ's sake! What could I have done differently so as not to have been shot at; not to have been a near-miss victim of a bombing; not to have had Jeff seek me out in what would be an obvious effort to persuade me to change sides?

Did I really want to rendezvous with a man who admitted he had been shot while breaking and entering? Not to mention a man who seemed constantly to put me in death's way.

Then, once again, why did Roxanne move me from the hospital to a house with a bugged phone?

I put in a call to Betty in New York. I wanted to make sure she knew where to come and pick up my body, if and when the situation deteriorated any further.

I was surprised that she already knew I was at the Litchi Klong house.

"Someone from Miss Whyte's office already called," she said. "Are you okay?"

Is the Pope a Protestant?

"Maybe you should come home."

Yeah, maybe.

Afterwards, I decided to test my legs. On cue, the houseboy stuck his head outside the door. "Anything wrong, Mr. Draqual?" Was his concern genuine, or was he instructed to make sure I didn't hop any boats sent by Jeff to ferry me across the klong?

"I just need a bit of exercise," I said. Dr. Changmai hadn't told me to walk marathons, but neither had she told me to stay immobile. A compromise seemed a logical solution for good health, especially if I wanted to be limber enough for any three o'clock boat ride.

I strolled the garden and periodically glanced toward the house to see what the servants were up to. They'd all disappeared but I was willing to bet the farm that if I called for a drink, the house boy would instantly materialize with one. Actually, a gin and tonic was something to keep in mind after I finished my brief reconnaissance.

How would it all play at three o'clock, as I bypassed flower arbors, skirted well-trimmed shrubs, slipped through the Litchi trees, and stepped onto an awaiting boat? Would I glance back mid-klong and spot someone in hot pursuit?

"B-movie scenario," I said to myself. Meaning not just the imagined scene, but my whole life back to and including the Slip to Die for murders.

I'd been in Bangkok numerous times, and nothing like this had ever happened before. Why had it happened this time? Jeff was the obvious catalyst. Everything and everyone was linked to Jeff. Jeff made Bangkok a place I could never again view with quite the same innocence. I wasn't sure I could forgive him for the way he'd tainted the environment.

I focused on the beauty and fragrance of the flowering frangipani. The flower's Thai name is lantome. Which sounds like ratome, the Thai word for "heartbroken". Bad karma, that! The tamarind tree, too, implies foreign influence. Mostly found cultivated in Buddhist temples, it isn't a tree any Thai would grow at home for decoration or shade.

I stopped at the Litchi trees. It was too early for Jeff's boat, so I peered through the leaves to the water, hoping for some trace of the bug I'd so carelessly discarded. The rotten odor of the klong was all I got.

I retreated to the far fresher air back at the table.

The houseboy appeared with a silver tray holding a Baccarat glass and pitcher. The latter was filled halfway with gin, tonic, and ice. Obviously, someone had bugged my mind, as well as the telephone.

"Would you please have someone get me a clock of some kind?" I asked. A travel clock was brought before I'd downed the last of my first glass of gin and tonic.

At lunch, there was a magical conjuration of cold pasta salad.

o o o

At 2:59, against my better judgment, I stood up, fully expecting that my doing so would bring the houseboy running. When it didn't, I was a little disappointed. A part of me wanted an excuse to miss my rendezvous with any Jeff-sent boat on the klong. While my personal impressions of Jeff remained positive despite everything, I knew from past experience that I couldn't necessarily rely upon intuition to identify crooks, liars, thieves, and other scoundrels. As for my heretofore sterling impression of Roxanne, it was tainted by her less-than-sterling performance when confronted with the possibility of fake bodhisattvas at the museum ... by the bloody bug in the telephone ... by my hazy memory of someone possibly having reported to her Jeff's shooting during his clandestine visit to the museum.

To make sure I didn't telegraph obvious signals that would bring the servants racing from the house, I paused at a small tree of scarlet hibiscus. Almost immediately, I wished I hadn't. Not because anyone appeared to notice or consider it suspect, but because the showy red flowers, once worn behind the ears of Thai executioners, are considered unlucky according to Thai superstition.

I checked my wrist for the watch that wasn't there. I didn't want to arrive at the klong early, or the boat wouldn't be there. I didn't want to arrive late, or someone might spot the boat and wonder about it before I boarded. All that said, I didn't want to walk around the garden with a travel clock, either.

I made directly for the Litchi trees and their part of the klong. The stench was overpowering as I pushed through the foliage and to the water's edge.

My timing couldn't have been better. The boat glided into place the moment I got there.

"Quickly, please!" the Thai boatman insisted. Actually, boat "boy" might be more apropos. He didn't look a day over ten. Like his small boat, which was far smaller than the infamous bullet-ridden water taxi on the Chao Phraya, his clothes were a shade of russet that matched the contaminated canal.

I clambered aboard and immediately the small craft angled its pointy bow toward the opposite embankment. There was no motor on this boat, and I suspected a desire for no noise had contributed to the decision to leave one behind. The kid's single paddle dipped silently to one side and then the other.

I sat cramped in the front, facing back toward the boatman and the shoreline that receded. My fanciful imaginings of this very scene made the reality anticlimactic—until a sudden disturbance, sounding very much like a bear barreling through the woods. An accompanying bellow, otherwise indecipherable, raised gooseflesh along my arms.

Roxanne's chauffeur, Nikolas, appeared through the Litchi. His dive was impressively graceful and stylish, worthy of an Olympic racer. He hit the surface, skimmed it, and kept right on coming.

I was spellbound by this fully-clothed man who braved the equivalent of an open-air sewer. I was more impressed as he began a skillful and graceful Australian crawl.

My boatman had turned back toward the noise to join me in my stare of utter fascination. Any paddling was completely interrupted. Only inertia kept the boat on course.

"Chawla! Chawla!" came shouts from the opposite shore. Maybe they identified the boatman. Maybe they merely meant, "Get a move-on!"

Jerked out of his reverie, my boatman returned to work with a vengeance.

I measured Nikolas' impressive gains. The boatman's best efforts would be hard-pressed to get us to shore before Nikolas got to us.

This wasn't the first time I'd seen someone brave the contaminated waters of a Bangkok klong. It was, though, the first time I'd seen a European do it. It all went back to generations of immunities built within the indigenous population. Thai children might swim klongs safely today, but only because their fathers, grandfathers, and great grandfathers risked their health swimming them yesterday. Nikolas isn't Thai. He's Swiss.

"Please, please!" the boatman literally screamed at me as our boat hit the embankment. He discarded his paddle by giving it a toss in Nikolas' direction. He rushed toward me. He stepped on my foot. Not even the pain of his weight on my instep distracted my attention from Nikolas who was quickly closing the distance between us.

Hands other than the boatman's roughly grabbed hold and unceremoniously jerked me bodily from the boat. "This way, please, Mr. Draqual."

I was literally lifted off the ground and carried to the taxi parked on the road adjoining the klong. I began to complain at being dumped like so much refuse inside the open back door of the vehicle, but it was short-lived. Sunlight glinted from the shiny black-metal barrel of the gun held, aimed in my direction, by the complete stranger in the cab with me.

"On the floor! On the floor! On the floor!" Three pairs of hands pushed and prodded, even as the door slammed shut from the outside. Something smelly and suffocating dropped atop me.

I was too furious, too battered, and too indignant to be scared. My position was awkward and cramped. The smells were of oil, gas, and rancid sweat. The taxi burned rubber and added that acrid stench and the dryness of thick dust to the already dis-

61

agreeable melange.

And where was Jeff? Had he conned me? Or, had these men, under Roxanne's instructions, done something to him?

Worst scenario of all, did these jerks plan to do something uncompromisingly nasty to me?

Before I allowed my vivid imagination to run completely amok, I reminded myself that Jeff, reportedly shot at more than once and wounded the last time, probably had every reason to come at this cautiously.

"Please listen carefully, Mr. Draqual," said my companion with the gun. "In a very short time this vehicle will stop, and I'll remove your blanket."

"Be sure to give it back to the goat it belongs to."

"When the blanket is removed, you are to sit up, get out of the car, and quickly enter the taxi parked directly opposite this one. Is that perfectly clear?"

"Is all of this cloak-and-dagger bullshit really necessary?"

"Do you understand the instructions?"

"Sure." I rallied at even the vaguest prospect of getting off the grubby floor.

As it turned out, I surrendered one grubby taxi floor for another. I surrendered one grubby blanket for another. Happily, though, the man with the gun stayed behind and left me alone, except for a driver.

Noises filled the air, and the car's progress became decidedly stop-and-go. At each stop I contemplated throwing off the blanket, opening the door, making my escape and ending the little farce.

"Uncover, please, and into the dress shop."

We had parked on a Bangkok street typically cluttered with sidewalk stalls and foot traffic. A driver whose car was blocked by my taxi honked his horn impatiently and screamed for us to get out of the way.

"Tell the clerk you've been sent by Mr. Montana, please."

Goddamn if we weren't using code words now; as if any juvenile couldn't make the connection between Billing and Montana, ergo (Jeff) Billing, Montana, for Christ's sake!

I got out feeling more than a little wobbly and ship-worn. No one here was likely to recognize the grease-stained ragamuffin entering this five-and-dime dress shop, as a famous designer of silken underwear for wealthy women.

A little old lady occupied a chair set so deeply among the clothing that I almost missed her. Hoping she heralded the end of my miserable journey, I said, "I'm from Mr. Jeff Billing Montana." She looked hopelessly confused, so I took pity and resorted to the correct version.

"Back door, there," she indicated with a shaky nod of her head.

"Right." Out the back door and into an alley. In the alley was a tuk tuk. On the tricycle end of the tuk tuk was another seemingly ageless Thai who could have been six or sixty. Maybe a slight exaggeration, especially as the man's bass-voiced, "See the sights?!" confirmed him as likely well into puberty.

Wearily, I climbed into the rickshaw portion of the tuk tuk and luxuriated in the comparison between it and the cabs I had ridden in to get there. I leaned back and stretched my legs. As soon as the tuk tuk entered the next thoroughfare, I spotted the Royal Hotel straight ahead. It was the only reference point I needed to tell me we traveled west on Rajadamnern Klang.

The tuk tuk turned left onto Ratchadamnoen Nai. I recognized the Premane Ground, where the weekend market was held.

After so much time under a blanket I found the present heat and humidity of the Bangkok afternoon far less oppressive by comparison.

Soon we were alongside the golden spires and decorative pavilions of the Buddhist Wat Phra Keo. My driver stopped at one gate. "There's still time for you to see the Emerald Buddha," he said.

As I walked away, I expected the driver to scream how I'd cheated him out of his fare. That didn't happen.

Eventually, I joined the line of devotees who carried flowers and stick incense into the covered gallery that surrounded the temple complex. When I looked back, my driver and his tuk tuk were gone.

I bypassed murals that depict scenes from the *Ramakien*, that Thai epic wherein Prince Rama's wife, Sita, is abducted by the demon king Totsakan. I looked expectantly for Jeff, but he was nowhere to be seen. Remembering the tuk tuk driver's reference to the Emerald Buddha, I continued with the crowd toward the entrance of the bot that housed the image.

I removed my sandals and went inside. The nave was dark, and it took me a moment to see the Emerald Buddha; a misnomer, really, in that it's carved from green jasper. In lotus-position, it crowns a multitiered ornate gilded altar. Worshipers in attendance bowed their heads toward the marble floor.

The smell and the smoke of incense made the enclosure claustrophobic. The candleflames, the only light in the room, flickered wildly. I tried to find Jeff in the dim light but couldn't. I waited for him to find me, and when he didn't, I grew more and more perturbed.

Reviewing everything that had happened to me, I wondered if I'd somehow been miscued as to directions.

Finally, the need for fresh air drove me outside. The cloying smells of cinnamon, flowers, sweat, frankincense and myrrh—a lethal combination if overdosed—wafted out with me. It took a full minute before I could breathe freely.

I found my sandals, jettisoned upon entering, and stepped into them. I crossed the flagstones and turned back to better see the massive enclosure. No sign of Jeff, only strangers, the library, the pantheon, the porcelain wiharn.

I wandered.

The tall chedi, bedecked in gold tiles, telegraphed reflected sunlight like a fourth-of-July sparkler. Automatically, my eyes closed to the flicker. When I opened them, I thought I caught a brief glimpse of Jeff.

I ascended the nearest stairway to the second terrace.

My exhaustion seemed so out of character I had to remind myself that I'd been in the hospital as early as that morning. I should be back at the Simms' lovely home, lounging in the Simms' lovely garden, and drinking the Simms' lovely booze served up by the Simms' skillful servants. It took a masochist to be here in compliance with Jeff's request. By rights, I should have headed right on down the stairs, out the gate, and hailed the first cab for four-nine-six Litchi Klong Road. Once at the house, I could apologize to Nikolas for having needlessly endangered his health in the fetid klong.

Instead, I went on up the steps that remained. At the top, I collapsed against the gilded statue of a claw-footed, spritely-tailed, half-woman, half-beast apsonsi.

Finally—"Hello, stud Stud," Jeff's by-now very familiar voice startled me from the shadow cast by the mythical gargoyle. I stepped into the muggy shade.

"You're bleeding!": my first observation. My second: "Obviously, you're not as good at breaking and entering as you are at causing trouble."

"Roxanne's calling it breaking and entering, is she?"

"She isn't calling it anything, at least not within my hearing."

Jeff is one of the few men I've ever seen who is actually handsome with a five-o'clock shadow. That day maybe it was the way his unkempt rugged good looks seemed to come so perfectly together: stubble, tousled hair, rumpled jacket, and the kind of pants with six pockets. All he needed was one of those French Army bush hats, with chin strap and pinned-up side, to make his ensemble complete.

"She doesn't know I overheard someone at the hospital mention you'd been shot during a break-in."

Nervously, he surveyed the immediate terrain. If any suspicious someone were suddenly to appear, Jeff was obviously ready to bolt. I wouldn't have been able to muster the sufficient energy to follow.

"How'd you find the bug on the phone?" he said.

"Someone rang me who introduced himself as 'Call-me-Kenneth-Critzer'..."

"That sleaze!" Jeff interrupted.

"You know him, then?"

"Oh, yes, I know him. A fellow soldier of fortune. Fewer of us around than some people may think. But what possible business can he have with you?"

"Seems he phoned to tell me he has something to sell me that will increase my life-span. He seems to think I'm as much on someone's hit list as you are."

"Did he tell you just how he figures that?"

"He was about to, before he recognized my phone was bugged. He rudely rang off before he got around to telling me."

The blood stain on Jeff's shoulder was getting bigger.

"Have you seen a doctor?"

"It's a clean wound." Which didn't exactly answer my question. "The bullet went in and out. Didn't hit any bone or damage anything vital. As soon as my body cooperates and replaces the blood lost, I'll be in great shape."

"I think you're still bleeding, or haven't you noticed?"

"I'm told that's to be expected. Maybe if we sit?" Without waiting for my reply, he slid down the base of the statue.

His head leaned back against the stone, his chin tilted slightly upward to put his Adam's apple in sexy high-relief. A drop of perspiration slowly traced the cleft in his chin. How salty, I wondered, was the taste of his sweat? How salty, I wondered, was the red of his blood?

"You really should see a doctor, if you haven't already." I sat down beside him and felt the heat radiating from his body.

"I'll be fine. Really."

"What am I doing here?" I asked myself, surprised I said it aloud.

"I asked you to come, remember? Open my upper-right jacket pocket."

The pocket flap easily lifted. I reached in and found several Polaroid snapshots.

The two statues, pointed out to me by Dr. Rangliti in the museum, were showcased in close-ups and long-shots. The architecturally distinctive interior was undeniably that of the Powell Whyte Memorial Museum.

"The statues are phonies," Jeff said. "I only had time to confirm the two, but I'd guess there are more."

He shut his brown—his chocolate—his mink-lashed—eyes. He swallowed. His Adam's apple slid up, then down. His neck muscles were noticeably corded. His mouth opened slightly. I waited for his pink tongue to moisten his ripe-to-pale-pink lips. I waited in vain.

"He was younger than you, but you have him beat all to hell in the looks department," he said.

I didn't have to be told; there was an awareness, osmosis-transmitted via our shared body heat, which told me without doubt that he referred to the Thai prostitute, Rhee Dulouk, whose tragic death had somehow started this all.

"His IQ couldn't have been all that high, either. But I was looking for a warm body, and his fit the bill. He tried to impress me with some stuff he'd picked up when he slept with a night guard at the museum. I've always been interested in Asian art, and what he said made me interested enough to ask to see him again. Which may have been all he was out for from the get-go. Only before we got around to seconds, he got his throat cut."

He swallowed again. The new movement, along the striated column of his throat, dislodged drops of neck-sweat and converted them into rills of moisture that glistened, like liquid gold, even in the shadows.

"Your Lt. Col. Chuab hasn't got a clue. He would prefer that the murder simply fade away. Maybe that would be my preference, too, if the kid hadn't managed to drag himself up one whole flight of stairs before he bled out in my doorway, in my arms."

He opened his eyes which were wet without tears. Brown-oh-so-brown eyes turned in my direction. And looked. Stared. Asked for what? Understanding?

He turned his eyes away. Again, he shut them.

"But, even if the statues are fake, why blame Roxanne?" I had to argue on her behalf. I owed her that much. "I don't see her motive when she proclaims, right along with the experts, Kan-buri and Rangliti, that the statues are real. All the advantages for her are if the opposite is proven."

I couldn't see any answer to that paradox. Was Jeff more insightful than I? Was he less caught up in the nuances of friendship and affection that made me unable to see Roxanne's complicity?

"Maybe I don't have the right answer," he said, "but ..."

He made me wait. I could almost see his brain working to sort out his thoughts and put them into some format I might be persuaded to understand.

A slight tic appeared along his left cheekbone. I had the nearly uncontrollable urge to reach out and touch his skin at that exact point, to feel the temporary spasms of his facial muscles. Would my touch break the tenuous tensile bonds that maintained his cheek's perspiration in beaded form? Could I make his sweat run down his face like it ran down his muscled neck? How sensuous would his skin be, sweat-damp beneath the caress of my fingers?

"What if Roxanne holds off on her claim that the collection should be hers by default, only so she can have her cake and eat it, too?" he said.

In my mind's eye, my roving finger encircled the jugular notch at the base of his neck and dipped into the pool of perspiration it cupped.

His brown eyes were suddenly open and back on me. I blushed with embarrassment. Was Jeff guessing my thoughts?

"It's hot," I said by way of lame excuse. An excuse which he seemed to accept at face value.

"If Roxanne keeps quiet for the moment, is it only because she wants it to look as if she's bending over backwards to cooperate with the Thai government?" That was the question he put to me. "That course of action prevents government interference with all the capital she has tied up elsewhere in the Thai economy. Whereas any impression she's unduly anxious to whip the collection out from under the Thai government could see the authorities retaliate and make trouble for her other business interests. If she clandestinely arranges for fakes to replace the originals, then tells the government she's prepared to keep the mysterious substitutions a secret so the Thai authorities can find the security breach and plug it, she's the good guy. If she arranges a seeming breach of museum security, and has it look as if I've sneaked into the museum, then tells the government she's willing to overlook even that foul-up in security, prepared to let the Thai authorities try to make amends, once again she appears to be doing her level best to stave off the inevitable."

I rephrased his insinuation as a question: "Roxanne arranged for you to breach museum security?"

"She could have made it easier for my contact at the museum to accept the bribe I offered him to let me in. And, she could just as easily have made sure someone was there with a gun the night I checked in."

"But even without Roxanne being involved, your contact was in a position to provide you access, yes?" I didn't like all of his could have this, could have that.

"Mahn Sutohn's a guard, isn't he? Who better to trust with knowing how security works? But why would he set up my murder when I was paying him so well?"

What kind of bribe had Mahn Sutohn been paid? Cash? Cock? I could easily imagine the museum guard with his pants down around his ankles, bent against a fake bodhisattva, fucked by a camera-clicking Jeff.

"How about that it's just physically impossible for Roxanne to get multi-ton fake statues into the museum and get multi-ton originals out?" I asked. "Especially since I've got the definite impression she's been left out of the loop, as far as specifics regarding museum security."

It all gave me a headache. It was all above and beyond me. How did I, someone who wouldn't know a fake bodhisattva from a real one if the latter jumped up and fucked me, get involved in all of this?

While on the subject of fucking, what in the hell was it with the heat, the humidity, my physical nearness to Jeff, and the slide-show of imagined fantasies playing in my head: Jeff fucking Rhee Dulouk, Jeff fucking Mahn Sutohn, Jeff fucking ... ? (Fuck you, Dr. Melissa!)

"What if the fakes were substituted as early as Los Angeles?" Jeff said.

God, but I wished the handsome butt-fucker would just shut up. I derived far more pleasure from just looking at him, just fantasizing about him, than in listening to him bad-mouth Roxanne, whom I'd known for years. I'd only known Jeff for days.

I liked Roxanne. I had genuine affection for her.

I wasn't even sure I liked Jeff Billing.

"Los Angeles?"

"The fakes arrive here. Roxanne says they're the real thing. Only later does she identify them as fakes and insinuates that they've been clandestinely replaced. Who but Roxanne and maybe a few others would know they were fakes all along?"

"How about Kan-buri? How about Rangliti?"

"Kan-buri has an expensive opium habit. Rangliti has two mistresses, plus a wife and three kids, all of whom live beyond their means."

Kan-buri has permanently drug-dilated eyes. Rangliti has a wife with a penchant for very expensive jewelry.

"Kan-buri's and Rangliti's vulnerabilities are possibly why they were brought on board in the first place," Jeff said.

I was hot. I was bothered. I was tired.

I was confused, because suddenly none of it needed to be as inexplicable as I'd originally imagined.

I resented Jeff and his possible solutions.

I resented his goddamn handsomeness. Probably with an elephant-size cock to boot.

I resented the possible complications all of this—Jeff right or wrong, whether I gave a rat's ass or not—could have on my relationship, personal and business, with Roxanne.

"Look, Stud," Jeff said, "someone has me by the balls and wants to squeeze the life out of them." A pretty picture, to be sure! "I can't help but think that someone is Roxanne. Would you, please, tell her what I think I have. I only ask that she meet me halfway and accept a mutually agreed-upon expert (preferably from outside Thailand), who can confirm all the collection statues are real or fake. You tell her that I plan to go public with what I have if she isn't prepared to give me a little something here."

Why in the hell didn't he tell her himself ... through the shrapnel of the next fusillade ... through the dust of the next bomb blast?

"So, how do I get back to you?" I needed a very cold drink.

"I'll be in touch. Just continue to check those phones for bugs."

"One more thing."

He waited.

"At the hotel, after the explosion, did you give me mouth-to-mouth?"

He laughed. It did nice things for his already handsome face.

"My lips to your lips—that's something we'd both remember, believe me."

He asked if I had money for a taxi. When I said no, he gave me some currency. I caught a cab to four-nine-six Litchi Klong Road. I watched the street signs: Sanamchi Road, Maharaj Road, Songwat Road, Rama IV Road. The city continued to emote disordered clutter, but its crowds miraculously thinned to nonexistence as the taxi turned into the more expensive living area that parenthesized Litchi Klong.

When the cab was three blocks from the entrance to the Simms' compound, on a street deserted except for a line of cars parked along each edge, I leaned forward and tapped for the driver to stop. "I'll get out here and walk the rest of the way, please." I needed some additional time to run over, in my mind, how (if?) I would approach Roxanne with all of this.

I was so consumed by my thoughts that I was completely taken unaware by the sudden metal against metal slide of a blue van side panel on my immediate right.

Foul-smelling dampness clamped my mouth and nose.

My serious struggles against my unseen attacker came way too late in the game.

My legs buckled.

I anticipated the sharp impact of my knees against the pavement. Instead, I experienced a brief floating sensation, followed by an inky oblivion.

11

Nausea gripped me. My head throbbed. I wanted to feel my forehead for any trace of a fever but I couldn't move either hand.

"Ah, how nice of you to join the party," someone said.

I didn't recognize the voice. When I opened my eyes, I couldn't identify the man who sat cross-legged on the mattress that covered the floor.

He was probably in his late sixties or early seventies. His white hair was a thin fringe around a completely bald pate. His face was all sharp angles and points, his cheeks hollow. His prominent Adam's apple punctuated a chicken-skinny neck that was encircled, but not touched by, a buttoned-up shirt collar. His tie was a nondescript strip of dirty yellow, open along its knot, and both of its ends trailed below the waistband of the man's soiled jeans.

"My name is Kenneth Critzer," he said, "and I have you handcuffed to the inside of my van."

My inner ear, as well as the constantly changing lighting (daylight, but which day?), told me the van was moving.

"This is one strange way to make your sales pitch," I said. We'd spoken so briefly on the phone at the house on the klong it was no wonder neither his voice nor my first glance provided recognition.

"I am sorry for the crude way in which you've been summoned to our little face-to-face, Draqual ..."

"Call me Mr. Draqual."

"Mr. Draqual," he said with a large dollop of sarcasm. "...but you rather took me off-guard. I was under the impression that you,

71

so recently out of your hospital bed, wouldn't likely be up and around, let alone out, quite so soon. That mistaken assumption on my part forced a bit of spur-of-the-moment improvisation. Luckily, no harm is done so far."

Harm, then, yet to be done?

"The exercise has been beneficial, however, as a perfect illustration of just how vulnerable you are, Mr. Draqual." He said the latter with trowel-it-on facetiousness. "Madam Elephant is far more adept at abductions than I am."

"Ah, yes, the illusive Madam Elephant, out not only to abduct me, I understand, but to kill me."

"Such a cavalier attitude will see your death accomplished far more easily than if you took the threat to heart."

"Why would Madam Elephant want me dead?"

I tried to find a more comfortable position, glad the soiled (God, with what?) mattress on which I sat was softer than the taxi floors to which I'd recently become accustomed.

"Madam Elephant wants you dead because of something that Rhee Dulouk heard from a museum guard. It's the same something that got passed on to Billing by Rhee Dulouk, during pillow talk. 'Pillow talk'—what a genteel way to say fuck and suck, wouldn't you agree?"

"Which may or may not explain why Madam Elephant, if there really is such a person ..."

"Oh, believe me, there is. You best bet is not to find out, up close and personal, just how real."

"... would possibly want Rhee Dulouk dead ... would possibly what Billing dead ... but why would she want me dead?"

"There's the general consensus that what was passed, via pillow talk, between the museum guard and Rhee Dulouk, between Rhee Dulouk and Billing, made a similar cross-over, via similar suck and fuck, between yourself and Billing."

"Suck and fuck ... Jeff ... and I?" I laughed sardonically.

"You deny his interest? You deny your interest?"

This guy needed enlightenment provided by a hearty blow to his head with a two-by-four! Just turn me loose. Just give me the two-by-four!

"I deny my interest."

He waited. He said, finally, "Which doesn't exactly answer all of what I asked you, does it?"

The guy not only looked like he hadn't been born yesterday (and hadn't bathed since birth), but that first impression, in his case, was the reality.

"You ever hear the expression, 'It takes two to tango'?" I said.

"Have you ever heard the expression, 'It doesn't take a genius to add up one and one and get two when a lingerie designer suddenly asks questions about the authenticity of pre-Ankor art'?"

As my German fencing master, sexy scar and all, used to say, "Touché!"

My body shifted, via centrifugal force, as the van rounded a corner.

"My apologies, by the way," he said, "as regards how I so rudely ended our little phone chat. I've grown more paranoid than usual, these last days, a little less able to access certain information sources, and I was given only your phone number, not the very important supplemental information that the phone belonged to Mr. and Mrs. Cecil Simms. Once that key fact became available ..." He left the thought unfinished, as if I were more than able to fill in the blanks. Wrong!

"Oh?" I tried, by way of encouragement.

"Most businessmen with residences in Thailand have all their incoming and outgoing calls automatically recorded for later replay nowadays," he obliged. "It's de rigueur as a way to monitor crank calls, ransom demands, death threats, and whatever else happens to come in over the phone lines. Killers and kidnappers are usually such volatile people. Actually, I wouldn't recommend involvement with any of this city's gangster element, on any level. They can be so horribly dangerous to one's health, if you get my drift."

"You mean, Cecil Simms bugs his own phones?"

"It's really quite logical, once you realize how much Mr. Simms is worth worldwide. On the other hand, I have come upon hard times, due to a recent business deal that's gone sour. It's very important to my continued well-being that I commence an extended vacation, far-far away from Thailand. Such a vacation requires additional bankroll to what I've presently at my disposal. Which brings me to the specific point of this sales meeting."

"Which brings you to this certain 'something' you have to sell me?"

"You would agree, would you not, that if you knew the identity

73

of Madam Elephant, it would be helpful as a means of keeping you out of harm's way?"

"You know who she is?"

"I'm just chock-full of information at the moment," he said.

"Verifiable information?"

"You didn't get rich by taking people at their word, I suppose?" He sighed, ham-actor-like.

"That bit of insight, and fifty cents, will get you a cup of coffee. What's to stop you from pulling a name out of a hat? I've always figured that's what the police do whenever they oh-so-conveniently provide identification for the latest top-man on the Thai underworld totem pole."

The metal cuffs were chafing my wrists and growing more and more uncomfortable.

"Oh, for the right price, I'm prepared to provide proof enough to impress even the police."

He pulled a vertically torn snapshot from his shirt pocket. I couldn't any more identify either of the three men candidly portrayed than I'd been able to identify the fake/real bodhisattvas.

"Which one is Madam Elephant, and how do I know for sure it's her?"

"Actually, Madam Elephant belongs right here," he said and flicked, with the tip of his right index finger, the torn edge of the photo. "But the missing piece of the picture will cost you."

My left leg had fallen asleep. I tightened my thigh muscles, then relaxed them, to stimulate circulation.

"Why don't you take what you have to the police?"

"Because the police can't possibly come up with as much money as you and Billing can." Which made me wonder why he didn't put the deal to Jeff. The question was written on my face more quickly and far better than had I put it into words.

"Granted, Billing has a nest egg he'd likely be ready to blow in order to find out the name of the certain someone who ordered Rhee Dulouk killed. But—according to my sources—the sum isn't nearly enough to get me as far away from Bangkok as I'll need be when the shit hits the fan. While his father is rich as Midas, the old man has been known not to come through for his son in the past. Billing Sr. is as straight as a stick and is unlikely to be interested in the skinny behind the death of some little Thai queer his son figuratively fucked to death. Last but not least, Billing presently seems the less likely of the two of you to be around for long. Depends, I guess, on just how accurate the shooter was the other night at the museum."

I was pleased Kenneth's information sources hadn't reported that Jeff was doing quite nicely, gunshot wound and all.

"Ask Lt. Col. Chuab about Kenneth Critzer," he said. "He'll tell you all about my dealings and suspected dealings in munitions. By now, he might even be able to tell you how I provided Madam Elephant with a certain Belgium shipment of guns. Guns that included the flawed rifle that saved Billing's and your sorry butts, down by the river."

"You supplied the weapon?"

"Oh, how quickly loyalties change in the sordid world of Thai crime! Did you, by the way, think to thank me for how I, however inadvertently, saved your life and simultaneously put my neck in the guillotine?"

"Hold your breath!" *Inadvertently* had been the key word. "Roll in the tumbrils!"

"Can you believe Madam Elephant somehow assumed I had test-fired every weapon in that deal? And now she's holding these couple of faulty rifles against me even more, because a couple other deals I brokered let faulty guns slip through, too. What if I'd been conscientious enough to test fire all of the ammunition? Do you think there'd have been a bullet left? Go figure!"

He checked his watch, probably not out of any concern that my hands and legs were about to fall off from lack of adequate circulation.

"You show Lt. Col. Chuab this part of the picture," he said and tucked what he'd shown me into my shirt pocket.

What with the Polaroids of the supposedly fake bodhisattvas in yet another pocket, I was beginning to feel like a scrapbook.

"You tell the Lt. Col. the photo was secretly snapped on Sangua la Grande."

"On Sangua la what?"

"It's a tiny island in the Caribbean. It was the location of a very private, and very secret, world-wide crime symposium held under the auspices of a certain Cuban gentleman. Part of the ten-day session included a detailed workshop on how to black market stolen

Third World originals and forged artworks, as a valid means to fatten any crime family's coffers. Madam Elephant was there."

Again, he checked his watch.

"Time does so fly as one gets older," he said; I agreed. Then, he quoted his asking price; I expressed my disbelief with wide eyes, with a dropped lower jaw, even (yes, I do believe), with an audible intake of breath.

"It's well worth the price, believe me," he said and patted me on the back. "Or do you figure your life should only be worth chicken feed?"

He provided the when-and-where of the proposed missing-picture-piece for money exchange. By which time, the van had maneuvered several more turns and come to a stop.

He uncuffed me and slid open the van door.

"This last bit is very important," he said. "You have my okay to get Chuab to confirm that I am who I say I am, and you have my okay to get to Billing to supplement the cash fund. Other than that, I want you to keep Chuab and Billing out of the loop. If I see Billing, the Lt. Col. or any cops at the exchange site, you can wave good-bye to the Madam Elephant photo-I.D. Understood?"

He actually waited for my reply.

"Understood."

He helped (read: pushed) me out and left me precariously balanced on tingling, half-asleep legs. Thus abandoned within an accompanying smoggy blanket of oily exhaust, I glanced around and realized I was pretty much back where I'd begun.

Tentatively, I took a first step toward the Simms' compound, whose couple-of-blocks distance now seemed like miles. I took a few more steps to assure myself of balance.

Nikolas waited just inside the front gate. I thought of a mumbled apology, since I had been responsible for his dip in the klong. However, as I hadn't really forced him to take his swim, I opted for no comment.

"Thank God!" Roxanne said by way of greeting my return. She had changed clothes since I'd last seen her and looked sophisticated in a white silk tuxedo. Her latest perfume successfully mingled musk, oak, leather, and smoke. "Are you okay?"

"I've seen Billing," I said. I took out the Polaroids of the purported fake bodhisattvas. "He says some museum guard, Mahn Sutohn, invited him into the museum to take these. He says the statues in the photos, which you, Kan-buri, and Rangliti claim to be genuine, are fake. He wants a mutually agreed-upon expert, not Thai-based, to settle the question. If not, he goes public with some story as to how you're out to keep the collection for yourself."

"Jesus!" That's what she said. Not, "What bullshit!" Not, "Crazy asshole!" Not, "The fucking lying bastard!" She punctuated this by dropping none too sophisticatedly, into a nearby chair.

"Roxanne?" Surely she could provide me with an explanation.

But "Christ, what a bloody mess!" was all she was able to come up with.

Roxanne wanted to meet with Jeff. She had to introduce him to "someone," she said. It might take time to set up, because this someone was presently out of town. Jeff should, please (she emphasized), be patient. He should do nothing until after they had talked. Roxanne would see that the meeting happened as soon as was feasibly possible.

"Do you want to give me a quick preview?"

"Of course, I want to." She kissed me on the forehead. "Of course, I can't. It all has to remain strictly need-to-know until later."

She left. She had to attend a party to which I wasn't invited. I would have been hard-pressed to go even if asked and fresh as a daisy. The festivities were put on by Denny Mullet (rhymes with sleigh) for Denny Mullet (rhymes with Hyacinth Bouquet). I'm talking a self-aggrandizing bon voyage party to precede a week of scheduled spelunking for Denny and a friend within the extensive newly discovered Panjumi cave network just a few miles drive southeast of the city.

Everyone knew Denny had taken up high-risk sports just because he thought it was the part of my background which made me particularly appealing to Roxanne. Before Denny and I met, he hadn't climbed a mountain, kyaked a river, or trekked the Inca Road.

As soon as I'd seen Roxanne off to see the lizard, I called Lt. Col. Chuab. He wasn't at his office. I left a message for him to get back to me.

I had a light dinner: arugula salad, white wine.

I had a long shower.

The Lt. Col. returned my call as I sat on the bed and prepared to fall back onto it.

"I'm just back from being kidnapped—chloroformed, gunny-sacked, and dragged into a van."

"You're okay?"

"It was some guy called Kenneth Critzer. He said you'd provide references."

"I do indeed know Mr. Critzer. He's a nasty piece of work."

"So, it would seem. He said he was 'in' munitions."

"We've nothing that can confirm that as true." He didn't sound even vaguely convinced. "Would you like to press charges?"

"My word against his, yes?"

"You have his bad reputation on your side."

"Would that be enough?"

"Most likely, especially if he made you stop off at your bank before letting you go."

"He wants to sell me a picture of Madam Elephant, taken on some island in the Caribbean, Sangua la something."

The Lt. Col. was dubious and insinuated Kenneth Critzer was not to be trusted. Chuab wanted to see the photo fragment. He'd send someone to get it.

"I'm literally on the bed, Lt. Col. My eyes droop as we speak. The next sound you hear will be my snores."

"I have a car in your area. It can be there in four minutes max."

It took five minutes. The courier was the same well-groomed lieutenant who'd dropped the file of Jeff (and my?) intended assassin on the Lt. Col.'s desk (how long ago was that?; it seemed years, but wasn't).

I was glad to see the photo gone. It was a police matter. I knew nothing about world-crime symposiums on exotic isles.

I lay back on the bed. I went to sleep.

My dream was erotic. Very. It was boner-producing. Very. It was nearly wet. Very.

All but an indefinable ghost of the dream, as well as my resultant boner, disappeared with the ringing. I cracked my sleep-glued lids. The absence of lighting in the room said morning would be awhile in coming. The ringing stopped. Maybe, it, too, was a nocturnal left-over: the last echo of some subconscious and automatic alarm system which had aborted something better-not-finished.

More and more often, I can't remember my erotic dreams, except that they are erotic. Once, I could not only remember them but, hand on hard cock, could fantasize their completion when they didn't quite get me to blast-off.

Now, though I wouldn't admit it even to myself, I was ill-at-ease over my drug-induced dream at the hospital. The dream in which Jeff Billing was naked, I was naked, and Jeff was up so close and personal that his hand almost touched the head of my erection. Drugs obviously had interfered with whatever natural defenses— internal ringing?—that normally would have unhooked that particular homo-eroticism from my subconscious.

I would have snuggled deeper into my blankets, had I had blankets. I had only one sheet and a cascade of mosquito net. Cuddling a lone sheet is a near impossibility.

I tried the mental game that supposedly resumes an interrupted dream. I imagined myself, standing, arms outstretched. I imagined I turned in tight circles, like a whirling Dervish. I went round and round and round and ...

There was a tap on the bedroom door. The door opened and the houseboy appeared.

Did he see my boner that cameoed the sheet as completely as Elgin Marble bas-reliefed its milk-cream stone? I would have made some effort to make my erection less obvious, but any such effort would merely have drawn more attention.

"Yes?" I attempted to deflect all his attention to my face.

"Miss Whyte called, Sir," the boy said. It was hard to see where his eyes focused. "She said she'll send the car around in an hour. You'll drive north, instead of taking the helicopter. So, she hopes for an early start."

"Thank you." I would have suffixed his name, had I known it. Why didn't I know it? Why had I never asked?

"Cook wonders what you prefer for breakfast."

"Just a couple of eggs, scrambled. Toast. Coffee."

"Should I lay out your clothes?"

"I'll manage my clothes and my shower, thank you."

Did he remain a few extra seconds beyond what was necessary?
Did he look at me, in general, or did he look, specifically, at the
ridge my hard dick made in the sheet?

"Jesus, Draqual!" I chided myself. "Get a grip!"

I would have liked a longer shower. I would have liked a more
leisurely jack-off. I would have liked a bit more time over my eggs,
my toast, and my coffee.

Nikolas opened the limousine door, and I—"What fun!"—
joined Roxanne within the car's luxurious interior.

The smoked glass that separated Roxanne and me from the front
seat was already up. The mechanically cooled air was aphrodisia-
cally afloat with the smell of expensive leather and yet another of
Roxanne's expensive perfumes.

"I figured if you were up to everything you were yesterday, a little outing today would be a piece of cake."

She wore a pale-blue silk mini-skirt, embroidery embossed with
understated dark-blue periwinkles. Her light-blue tailored jacket had
the same dark-blue embroidery on its lapels. She wore no blouse but
showed, instead, the upper half of her powder-blue Draqualian-silk
slip. Along its low-cut bodice rode periwinkle lace in dark-blue
Draqualian silk thread. It was an outfit she must have worn especially for my benefit, because it would have raised eyebrows in
public. Thais, in general, still remain a tad conservative in dress.

"Love your outfit," I said.

"I thought you might."

Did she know the first person to appear in public in just a
Draqualian slip was a drag queen?

"I'm always tempted, whenever I see anyone wear your underwear as outerwear," she said, "to walk up and say, 'My dear, you
do know a drag was there long before you were, don't you?'"

Possibly, an indication of our shared empathy: how easily she
reads my mind.

What didn't require telepathy was her follow-up, "Do you have
a couple of frolicking ferrets in your pants pocket, or are you just
happy to see me?" It wasn't something she would have said B.J.
(Before Jeff). Which provided one more disruption of my life for
which I could give him credit (blame?).

My monkey, strangled in the shower less than an hour before, proceeded all the more quickly toward full tumescence. My prick always conducts itself as if it has a life completely separate from my brain. I take a great deal of masochistic satisfaction in how I've finally managed not to let it, hard or soft, lead me around by the crotch.

My dick might not be large, but what it lacks in inches, it always makes up for with mendacity. More than once, knowing exactly what I have between my legs, and wishing desperately for more, I've still been impressed by the invitation one of my boners offers while in my pants. Often, I'm not the only one impressed.

"I've never met a man so often, so easily, sporting a hard-on," she said.

"It's the ultimate compliment on how you look," I said. It had worked before.

It didn't work now.

"Come on, Stud, do give me credit for having been around the block at least a couple of times."

Of course she was right. What kind of compliment is it when my cock gives the same automatic response to a knothole?

"It would be easy for a woman to think so, though," she said, "if she didn't know better. I've no doubt it's magic that, more than once, has proved to your advantage in business. Do you think your ablility to fuck anyone, anywhere, any time, is a hereditary thing, passed on from father to son?"

I don't remember that my father walked around with a perpetual hard-on. But there's a lot of things I can't recall. (Anyway, that's what Dr. Melissa constantly insinuates.)

"I remember my father as being strictly monogamous," I said. "But, then, I only knew him after he'd met and married my mother."

"Maybe it's one of those things that skips a generation," she said.

"Do we really want to spent the morning discussing my penis?"

She laughed.

"I like that you make me laugh," she said. "I like that you're charming and sophisticated. I like that you've the good looks to stop a runaway freight train. I like that your cock goes hard whenever you see me. It's all a very attractive package for an astute businessman."

"I don't think of our relationship as purely business," I said. I meant it.

"I know you don't," she said. "If you did, I wouldn't have thought of you, first thing, when the initial green-dyed silk came out of the dyeing vat."

She leaned over, took one of my hands, and squeezed it. She put it to her cheek. Her eyes locked on mine, and she turned my hand over and kissed its wrist at the base of my palm.

"You're a genuinely sweet man."

A man who still had the occasional ability to blush.

"Trust me," she said. "Whatever doubts you may now have about me will all work out."

She let go of my hand. Pensively, she turned to the window.

The last edges of Bangkok's urban sprawl exited the landscape around us. We were entering a world possibly unchanged for hundreds, even thousands, of years.

"My biological clock ticks extra loudly, as of late," she said but kept her focus out the window. "Do you ever think of having children?"

"Of course, I 'think' of having them."

"And?"

"And, at this point in my life, I think I'd make a less than ideal parent." (Dr. Melissa, I'd bet money, would whole-heartedly agree.)

Water buffalo grazed the field outside.

"I don't necessarily look for someone who professes to be, or would be, an ideal father," Roxanne said. "Although I wouldn't be satisfied with someone only in terms of a few squirts of sperm, either, whether those squirts swam directly for my egg, or got there indirectly, via some petri dish. Certainly, I don't want to rely upon the word of some financially involved doctor, no matter his credentials, to assure me that the DNA, frozen in some laboratory test tube, is donated by someone charming, handsome, and witty."

Not that far distant were some of the world's few remaining original-growth jungles. Wherein an occasional elephant (other than the Madam) still harvests wind- or man-toppled timber, and . . .

Roxanne turned in my direction. "We head dynasties, you and I," she said. "Does either of us want his or her blood-line to end, just because we can't find Mr. or Ms. Right? What empire builder of the past would have been stopped by a little thing like the absence of love? A way would simply have been found to work around it. Should you, should I, be any different?"

... tigers still prowl shadowy ground level and occasionally turn man-eater.

"Are you asking me to marry you?" My voice actually cracked. I was wondering if things would have come to this if Roxanne hadn't felt our relationship had been somehow altered by the appearance of Jeff .

"My only proposal, at the moment, is that you think of the possibilities," she said. "Whether I'm ready to take it farther is dependent upon just how much louder and faster my biological clock ticks."

I didn't ask her if she had discussed any similar baby-making options with Denny Mullet (maybe before he headed off for spelunking?). I gave her more credit than that, even though she'd never gone out of her way to dissuade him from his perpetual mating dance. (Did she find his courtship as flattering as I found it fawning? Did she use it as a tool to make me jealous?). Okay, maybe I didn't ask because I didn't want an answer that might shatter my assumptions. On the other hand, nowhere in her criteria for a suitable sperm doner had she included "short and a poor loser". And there could be no denial of potential benefits to me and to mine, to her and to hers, from our linkup. Just the combination of our respective silk-production companies, with her contacts in the Orient, and mine in the Americas, would make a power-house to be reckoned with within the industry. And Roxanne had more than just a silk company. She headed a virtual conglomerate. If she succeeded in retaining possession of her uncle's Thai art collection, despite all of Jeff's efforts to the contrary, she'd have those additional assets in the millions of dollars. Even if Roxanne and I didn't officially tie the knot, and she preferred to raise our child on her own, our kid would reap a plentiful harvest from the bargain.

Of additional advantage would be the resulting silence of my mother's final mantra of the trio of mantras she chanted for years: "Stud, please quit all of this dangerous polo playing, river-rapid riding, mountain climbing, what-all, before you get yourself killed."—"Stud, please take more notice of your father's business which, after all, will be your business some day."—"Stud, please give me a grandchild."

"Just give me a little forewarning when and if you ever want to take this any farther," I said.

There was no need to get down to specifics as long as the project was speculative and/or on hold. As for my fulfilling my physical part of any such deal, I had no doubt it could be done. I'd fucked plenty of women I didn't love, most of whom I had less affection for than I had for Roxanne. I've always been good at performing the mechanics of the sexual act, though somehow I never seem to get beyond the mere mechanics.

"How about a drink?" she said. "It's never too early for champagne."

Knowing a bottle-on-ice was likely no greater distance than the limousine wet bar, I said, "I'd love a glass."

It turned out to be an excellent-year-vintage Dom Perignon that went down easily and tasted exotically of oak. Minute bubbles seemed to effervesce the very crystal of my fluted tulip-stem glass.

"To business and to friendship," Roxanne said.

"To business and to friendship," I agreed.

The scenery changed to central plain. Stretched out on either side of the road were mile after mile of rice paddies. The slick surfaces of the many flooded squares reflected, then didn't, sunlight. It was as if green-Plexiglas tiles of a disco dance floor, extended to each horizon, were continuously and randomly hit with light from above or below.

"I hope you're not too disappointed by my decision to drive this time," Roxanne said. "It takes longer than by helicopter, but it gives me a feel for the country that I like to renew on occasion."

In another day and age, I might have suspected her of trying to isolate me from Jeff until she had time to arrange for their intended meeting. But as it was, the car had a cell phone. Jeff was ingenious enough to access the number.

"I'm delighted you decided to drive," I said. Roxanne was easy to look at. Our conversation was enlightening and interesting. The accommodations were luxurious; the plush leather was a welcome nest for my still weary and aching bones and muscles. On and off, I dozed. The last time I came awake, I automatically looked at my wrist for the time. I still hadn't replaced the Piaget that had been broken on the river.

"It's a little before eleven," Roxanne said. "I've okayed a brief detour, since we have the time. I would have gotten your input, but you seemed so ... so ...."

She caressed the glass she held. Her hands aren't likely to be seen in any moisturizer commercial. They're small and quite squarish. Her nails, clipped functionally short and almost always without embellishment beyond their buffed glossy shine, provide windows on perfectly half-moon cuticles. Her fingers, at least against the slightly off-white of the champagne, were surprisingly pale for having spent so much time exposed to the debilitating sun of the tropics.

"Has anyone ever told you how genuinely angelic you can look when you're asleep?" Roxanne said.

"Not recently." How long had it been since I'd taken someone—anyone—to bed with me? It had been so long that my younger, more promiscuous self, would have felt positively deprived. "What kind of a detour?"

I was answered not by Roxanne but by the appearance of a house, off to one side. We'd driven into an area devoid of rice paddies but scattered with tall and stately palm trees. The ground shrubbery was low-growing and luxuriously green.

We drove the road that meandered toward the house.

We passed a lone farmer who hoed the already turned-up soil within a small plot of ground.

Unlike the Simms' compound, this residence was typically Thai, raised on poles to protect it from floods. Its steeply slanted roof, punctuated with ngaos, was designed to shed rainwater.

We pulled up in front and parked directly opposite a flight of wooden steps topped by a closed wooden gate. Roxanne and I (Nikolas remained with the car) were given the traditional wai greeting by the pretty young girl who opened the gate without a summons. We were ushered onto a large elevated veranda. To our right was the larger of two wood-paneled structures. We headed left to the smaller, whose panels, miniatures of their mirror-image companions, stood open.

Coming in from the bright sunshine, I found it difficult to see. My first impression was of a shadowy space thoroughly draped in cobwebs. Like a spider, an indiscriminate "something" waited within.

As soon as my eyes adjusted, I more accurately identified the wind-blown gossamer as intricately exquisite lacework. The lone occupant was an elderly woman in a high-back chair. On the woman's lap was a bobbin-strewn pillow. By the way she unstuck several of the remaining pins as we approached, I could tell her latest tatting project was completed. She continued detaching the resulting lace from the paper pattern that was attached to the pillow.

"Stud Draqual, I'd like to present you to Mrs. Emily Trang."

"Sammy Ped Mai's grandmother?"

"Sammy!" The old lady frowned. She actively spat.

"Best not to mention Sammy ..." Roxanne said, the tip of her index finger dimpling her already pursed lips.

"Sammy!" exclaimed the little old lady with an accompanying dry hack.

"... except in the third person," Roxanne finished with a small smile. "Mrs. Trang and he definitely do not get along, for all the reasons I mentioned earlier."

"Your work is exquisite, Mrs. Trang," I said.

Some of the tatting had to have required over a thousand bobbins. Although the old lady's bobbins, from her latest project, showed individual designs to help her keep them separated, I couldn't imagine myself trying to memorize the what, the where, and the when of over a thousand of them.

The old woman smiled widely and revealed one very bright gold incisor.

Her neck scarf was vintage Hermes. "Summer bouquet": sunflowers, daisies, mums, irises, all in varying shades of yellow against a richly buttery silk background; it draped her neck Boy Scout style, attached in front by one of the 24-carat slip-knots made famous, in the late sixties, by Tiffany designer Rolph Jaganell.

She plucked the remaining couple of pins from the pattern and its supporting cushion, and she held the lace up for me to see. It was a gauzy six-pointed star, truly lovely.

I wondered how I could finesse this woman out of several pieces of her work for incorporation into the several new Draqual lingerie designs which spontaneously leapt into my mind.

"Mr. Draqual mentally calculates how much money he'd have to pay to buy you out, Mrs. Trang." Roxanne hit the nail on the head.

The old woman said something I'd never be able to translate in a hundred years and cackled like a hen. Her head bobbed like a bobbin.

"Unfortunately," Roxanne said and turned to me, "all of these pieces, including the one just finished, have already been spoken for. And, as Mrs. Trang's presently improved financial situation no longer requires her to work for a living, the only tatting she does now is for gifts."

"I'm rather disappointed you didn't call her to my attention long before now." My disappointment was genuine. I saw workmanship that provided true inspiration, and I was naturally beset by a kid-deprived-of-his-candy pique.

"I only just became aware of her myself, as a result of some scheduled lumbering."

"Okay, you managed to save your beautiful you-know-what on that count. Surely, though, she must have one or two pieces to spare."

"For being such a good sport, I'll see what I can do by way of a consolation prize."

On cue, the old lady rifled a stack of lace on a nearby table and pulled out a small square of green latticework whose one end tumbled floorward into six feet of lacy silk ladder perfect for lingerie trim.

"How much?" I didn't know whether to address the old lady or Roxanne, so I spoke into the air between.

"On the house," Roxanne said.

"A gift," the old lady insisted. Her arm pushed and pulled her handful of lace at and from me, as if each push somehow got it closer.

Beware of Greeks bearing gifts? Beware of Roxanne and an old Thai woman bearing lace?

"Gee!" I said.

"I truly love your knack for expressing appreciation, like an innocent little boy," Roxanne said; I replayed what she said for sarcasm but only detected amused irony. "Too many men too soon lose it." She sounded quite serious.

I took the lace before the offer was rescinded. The filigree of super-fine silk threads was as gossamer as cotton candy. I refolded it neatly and put it in the top front pocket of my Brioni safari jacket.

"In afterthought ..." Roxanne started.

Few things in life come without a price tag, and I arched my eyebrow as I waited to hear the real cost of this one. I reminded myself that the two women would be hard-pressed to wrestle the lace from me. However, if they called upon Nikolas...

"... tell Sammy Ped Mai ..."

"Aghrr, Sammy Ped Mai, ptui!" said the old lady with an accompanying dry hack.

"... that I've not made off with his grandmother. Quite to the contrary, I'm keeping her safe and well-protected from the likes of him."

The only difficulty I had with that, although I promised it to her on the spot, was that I certainly had to take her word as proof-positive for the statement just made. For the little old lady before me in no way resembled the tree-hugger Nana in the photograph Sammy showed me in the lobby of The Oriental Hotel.

My dilemma wasn't new. It had happened at Groton whenever two students were chosen by the coach as captains to pick relay swim teams from the rest of us. I (all my usual modesty aside) was the best swimmer my class had to offer. So much so, I was never faced with that school-boy trauma, "Please don't pick me last, yet again!" Mine was always, "Gee, I like the captain of the blues. Gee, I hate the captain of the reds. Please, God, let the captain of the blues win the toss to pick me first." My like or dislike of the captains seldom had anything to do with the moral turpitude of either, or lack thereof. Tony Granston cheated on every exam, and everyone but the faculty knew it. Gyle James was a Boy Scout who remains, to this day, the only person I ever saw help an old lady across the street. I thought Toby was an A-OK guy. I thought Gyle was more odious than cat shit.

Now, the captains were Roxanne Whyte and Sammy Ped Mai. I liked Roxanne better. Her business interests were tied to mine. She'd asked me to consider fathering her child. Did I care that she kept secrets from me about whatever was or wasn't going on at the museum? Did I care that she lied to me about Sammy's Nana? Did it matter why she felt she couldn't trust me, why she lied to me? Damn right, it mattered: Just how much I cared, just how much it mattered, we all had to wait and find out.

We passed the same lone farmer, in his small plot of turned dirt, on our way out. If I didn't know better, I would have guessed he'd moved no more than a couple of feet. Probably, he was slowed by the heat. Sometimes I forget it's far more difficult to work in the Thai sunshine than it is merely to pass through it on the way from one spot of shade or air-conditioned space to another.

I tried not to let my consternation over the possibly fake bodhisattvas and definitely fake Nana spoil the rest of my day. I always enjoy my visits to the Whyte silk-production facilities. They provided an eclectic hodgepodge of old and new, ancient and modern. It's a welcome variety far more interesting and attention-getting than the thoroughly sterile environment that results from the more strict safety and labor regulations I deal with in New York State.

In Thailand, whenever "to modernize or not to modernize" comes up for debate, the scales are almost always tipped in favor of the status quo. That's because Thailand still has, as a natural resource, its enormous work force. The countries of the Western world long ago pretty much depleted theirs.

My tour was prefaced by our picnic at one of my favorite spots at that particular facility. Its intimate Thai pavilion sits on the crest of a grassy well-manicured hill overlooking the antiquated baths in which dyes are still set in cloth by running water. Only here have I come across this ancient holdover, usually replaced, elsewhere, by less labor-intensive simple dips in chemical baths.

The idea is to secure a color so completely that it doesn't run once in the hands of the buyer and/or designer.

For this purpose, river water is pumped into a large reservoir and funneled, via a short man-made riverbed, into six forking man-made streambeds. The latter align, side-by-side, within a stretch of land situated between a graceful meander of the Menam. The end results are six charming little cascades that return water to the original source, only downriver. From the picnic spot on the hill, there is a non-stop view of the six aligned streambeds, the riverbed, the spillway, the reservoir, and the river that arches the whole in seeming protective custody.

What made the spot particularly enchanting, on that particular day, were the six washed lengths of yardage, one color for each streambed. Whether by chance or by circumstance, the colors of the silk were the colors of the spectrum: red, blue, yellow, violet, green, orange. The green was the very same originally bled from the bruised petals of those tiny orchids. The whole made an exquisite rainbow that rippled sensuously and provided continually subtle changes of tint because of the water, because of the movement of the water, because of the sun, because of the movement of the sun, because of the clouds, because of the movements of the clouds.

We snacked on miang kham of ginger, coconut, lemons, red onions, dried shrimp, peanuts, and syrup sauce. As well, there were intricately and exquisitely carved vegetables: chrysanthemums from scallions; roses from radishes; additional flowers from carrots and chilies. There was a satay of pork slivers and cold khao na pet of roast duck laid out on a tray encircled by folded cucumber leaves. For dessert, we had a wide selection of luk club, a rare treat of delicious sweet meats made to resemble miniature vegetables. With all this, we drank bia poured into Baccarat wine glasses. The beer tasted hearty and robust after the champagne we'd indulged in en route.

Fifteen minutes into the meal, Roxanne took a call on her cell phone and was informed of some kind of glitch in the security system along the wall enclosing the entire grounds. Fifteen minutes after that, a second call informed her that the problem was solved. When I pressed her for details, after much coaxing she reluctantly explained: "Sorry, while you're eating, but it seems some cat got electrocuted and screwed up a few circuits."

My ensuing tour of the facility wasn't an in-depth first-timer's look. I'd been there plenty of times, and my walk-through was geared toward acquainting me with changes since my last visit.

As usual, I found the on-site silkworms of particular interest, in that the worm farm they comprise is purely experimental. Whyte Silk's major worm farm is farther northeast. The mulberry tree, whose leaves are most silkworms' sole food supply, is better adapted for conditions at higher elevations than those of Thailand's central plain. The plain site was selected because of its nearness to Bangkok and all the advantages that hub offers for disbursement of the finished product to markets worldwide. So, spools of raw silk thread are shipped daily from the more mountainous northeast to the lower southern facility, where they are graded and woven into cloth. The purpose of the worms at the plain site is to experiment with silk from an indigenous lowland mutant mulberry tree. Both worm and mutant tree populations were much enlarged since my last visit. The quality of the resulting silk was improved, but it was still inferior to that produced by worms and trees farther northeast. Nonetheless, Whyte Silk has a market for the plain-produced silk: developing countries with the taste for luxury but not yet with the pocketbooks to afford the very best.

Trays of silkworms waited to be hatched.

Larger bamboo trays contained hatched worms growing into larvae state while glutting on a constantly replenished locally grown food supply.

Fully developed silkworms settled down within circular bamboo trays with frames that left just enough space for each worm to attach its cocoon.

Single-thread cocoons were dropped into pots of water heated to just below the boiling point. This not only kills the worm inside, but it releases the silk thread for unwinding. Each result is either individually rewound on a spool, or first twisted with other strands for rewinding. Silk from the outer layers of a cocoon provide the coarser yarn for use in home furnishings. The silk that's my bread and butter always comes from the softer, very inner layers.

In one large shed, the largest under-roof acreage on site, women were busily weaving the silk on upright looms with foot treadles.

I spent several minutes watching a virtual crowd of young women finishing final preparations of the yardage I'd requested for green tie-dye. Some women gathered up large and small bits of the material and tied those off. Other women worked parts of the material into intricate pleats and folds. Other women sewed various size objects—from single rice grains to small groupings of glass marbles—into the material. All to achieve diverse, and usually quite lovely, color patterns once the material passed through the dye vat to accept or reject coloring—dependent upon how it was planned for this stage of the process.

My last stop was the large barn-like structure that housed the dyeing vats. Roxanne and I were accompanied by Krath Sabop. Over the years, Mr. Sabop and I have become quite good friends, even though, as Whyte Silk's chief dyeing expert, he is forever trying to get me to reveal how my grandfather, my father, and now I, manage to make our silkworms secrete silk already colored within their digestive tracts. Mr. Sabop always has a new tale of woe regarding his attempts to get some of Whyte Silk's worms to excrete multi-colored threads—with disastrous results. This time was no exception.

"We're lucky to have a silkworm left alive," Roxanne joked, right on cue.

"No, missy," Mr. Sabop insisted, as he always does. "I use only a few. Only a very few."

Mr. Sabop was most anxious to show me Whyte Silk's latest addition. Surprisingly, it wasn't the impressive steel vat which Roxanne had okayed to keep certain key company employees aware of the latest technological advances in the field. Rather, it was an adjoining vat whose on-the-scene construction had been overseen by Mr. Sabop.

"It cost much less. It works much better," said a beaming Mr. Sabop.

I concurred with him entirely on his first estimation; it looked thrown together from cheap pieces salvaged from some local scrap heap. As for the "much better" he boasted, I had my doubts, though I pretended to admire it.

"Actually, it does work," Roxanne said. She sounded as if she, too, had once believed it wouldn't. When Mr. Sabop turned aside briefly to reprimand some poor kid with a mop for some imagined or minor infraction, Roxanne turned to me and whispered, "At least it worked that one time."

"Go up top," said Mr. Sabop, once he'd assured himself his mop-boy was back to his boss's high standards. "Go see." He waved us in the direction of the stairway that climbed the vat's circumference in a rickety helix.

Roxanne's expression said, "It's entirely up to you, Stud."

"Okay," I said, as if there were too few dangers in my life now that I'd given up polo, white-water rafting, and mountain climbing. However, when I headed up the stairs, Roxanne immediately behind, I was curious to see Mr. Sabop head in another direction.

"Beware of bald hair stylists, fat dieticians, dentists with false teeth, and," I stated ominously, as I paused before I took another step, "vat builders who flee their own constructions."

"He's off to read a voluminous array of disks and dials to assure a fault-free show," she said. "I can only repeat, as someone who's been here before, it worked perfectly the last time."

Up we went, each stair protesting our weight. Finally, we exited onto the small platform that overlooked the lip of the tub. Below, a series of large paddles protruded inward from the sides of the metal hole. I felt positively Lilliputian. Everything was shaking. I pulled back from the railing—which seemed insufficient on any account—for fear the vibrations would jiggle me right on over.

Roxanne, made braver by way of her previous experience, hung daringly over the balustrade.

"Liquid incoming," she said.

With a sound more likely to accompany a tsunami, water gushed. Paddles quickly submerged but made their presence known with additional noise, vibrations, and a sudden roil of liquid into more five-class white-water than any rapids I'd ever run. The influx of bile-like dye was fascinating to watch. Merely a small jet stream of the green diffused quickly to taint all previously colorless fluid.

I was so hypnotized by the conversion of color within the dyeing vat, it was only by chance that I shifted my attention from the noisy show to the comparatively noiseless black-hooded figure who sped up the stairs, two steps at a time.

With a totally spontaneous reaction my body pivoted to the left, my right leg lifted, my right foot rode its glancing blow along the oncoming man's ribcage. He made a grab for my leg on the way by, and missed, only to snag Roxanne's jacket. The knife blade suddenly visible within his free hand flashed warning like a lighthouse strobe, as his continued momentum torqued me into an even more pronounced pivot.

He struck the edge of the vat railing, and went over.

14

Roxanne teetered. Her feet tipped off the ground from the pull of the man's weight. I wrapped my arms around her waist and held on. That the seams of Roxanne's jacket held longer than the man's clutching fingers is a testament to the staying power of bespoke stitching.

I knew the moment he was gone, because Roxanne went featherweight. My ongoing attempt to keep her anchored brought us both down. For a horrifying instant, I thought we'd slip into the vat beneath the railing. Then, just when I was confident I had Roxanne safely secure, the vat went grand-mal. Gears groaned. Dead-weight shifted. Multi-ton metal, water, dye, Roxanne, I, and seemingly everything around us, performed a dance-macabre. Mr. Sabop arrived and performed a precarious weave of his own at the top of the stairs.

The cataclysm stopped, the sudden silence deafening.

"I saw the bastard run up," Mr. Sabop said. Cautiously, he stepped to the edge of the cauldron and peered into it. He turned back to us. "Every sign said someone had gone in. I feared it was one of you."

"Every sign"? Jesus! How many times had he been provided with bases for comparison?

"Is the shit dead?" I asked.

"Oh, yes, I do think so," Mr. Sabop said. "I've never seen anyone survive a mangling between paddles to the point of gear gridlock."

The only thing I could do was something I hadn't done in years. I started to (yes, goddamn it!) cry. No matter that I recognized the picture was all wrong: the hero falling apart; the heroine consoling with, "You saved our lives, you saved our lives, you saved our lives."

It was how I'd saved our lives, by ending the life of another, that didn't seem to compute. I'd taken karate as a precaution, but I'd never expected to put it to death-dealing use. Actually, I'd been relieved when my G.P. suggested it might be better, after my polo accident, to stop the joint-taxing karate altogether. Granted, my inadvertent experiences with mayhem and murder in New York City had seen me connected with one murder victim after another, but I hadn't been responsible for any of them.

"It's only natural, what you feel." Roxanne said. "You just have to remember, it wasn't something you did because you liked doing it. You were forced into it."

I barely made it to the edge of the vat before projectile vomiting my picnic lunch. My green-dyed dead-Thai manslaughter-victim would hardly gave a damn with what additional messy shroud I covered him.

I'd hardly wiped the last of the vomit from my mouth with the tissue Roxanne gave me before the local police investigation of the incident was over. At least it was pretty much done as far as I was concerned. Inspector O'Reilly, NYPD, would not have been impressed by how unprofessional it was. My part consisted of nothing more than looking green around the gills while Roxanne gave a terse synopsis of events.

"The would-be assassin came at us. Mr. Draqual came to the rescue."

The policeman left.

"I've ordered the helicopter to fly you back to Bangkok," Roxanne explained to me. "I'll tie up loose ends here."

"They won't need me?" I was mentally and physically distraught but still resentful of being moved one more step away from even a half-ass investigation.

"Lt. Col. Chuab will be arriving on the chopper."

Another crime overlapping areas of influence and requiring Chuab's liaison?

"The Lt. Col.'s from around here," Roxanne said. Which insinuated all sorts of possible (probable?) Roxanne-Whyte Silk/Lt.- Col. Chuab connections.

"It'll all be fine," she reassured me. "I owe you big time."

I didn't ask, "Do you owe me big-time enough to tell me more about Jeff's accusations, and why you lied to me about Sammy Ped Mai's grandmother?" That I could just as easily have been the one who ended up mix-mastered in the dyeing vat put all of those questions on some entirely unretrievable level of my psyche.

Roxanne left me in a small office near the heli-pad, promising that she'd be back to see me safely off. Until then, there were things she had to do.

"Anything I can do?"

"You've done enough already." She kissed my forehead, ran her fingers through my hair (punctuated with a tousle), and left me with a Styrofoam cup of hot, black coffee. Where were the Baccarat tulip glasses?

God knows how long I sat there, completely unfocused. Eventually the reality of the office space penetrated my inner fog. File cabinets were all perfectly aligned. None of the pictures on the walls were in the least bit crooked. The corners were free of cobwebs. Not one dust-bunny peeked from beneath the desk. Stacks of paper, wherever placed, were so precisely tiered they might have been contained within invisible boxes. In my recollection, only the

Bangkok police department office in which I'd first met Lt. Col. Chuab could claim similar fastidiousness.

The young man who entered the office pushed one of the buttons on the desk console and further interfered with the room's pristine otherworldliness by carrying the phone over to me.

"An incoming call, Mr. Draqual," he said. "We picked it up in the other room."

I wasn't surprised to hear Jeff on the other end of the line.

"Roxanne needs a couple days," I said in monotone. "Someone you need to meet isn't available until then."

"Your take on her story?" Jeff's voice, low, mellifluous—more importantly, so damned confident and in control—made me strive for the same.

"She never told me a story."

"She seems sincere?"

"Yes."

"Are you all right?"

"Why?"

"You sound funny."

"It's not been one of my best days, Jeffy." Jeffy?

"So, I'll give her a couple of days."

"There has been another development," I said.

"Oh?"

"Kenneth Critzer, wants to sell me a photo of Madam Elephant." I wearily provided the details up to the point where I had handed over the partial photo to Lt. Col. Chuab.

There was a pause.

Finally Jeff said, "I wish you'd given that picture to me."

Too damn bad! Obviously, it was a police matter.

"Chuab thinks Critzer's full of shit," I said.

"Nonetheless."

Moving right along ...

"You have connections, right?" I said. "Otherwise, you'd be run to ground by now."

"Maybe I know a few people. Why?"

"Do you know anyone who might tell me anything about Sammy Ped Mai?"

"Who?"

"Sammy Ped Mai. A prostitute-pimp who swears Roxanne made off with his grandmother, Emily Trang."

Maybe that, too, was something better left handled by Lt. Col. Chuab. My mind was still scrambled, and I wasn't sure whom I'd told what.

"Where in the hell did you hear that?" His tone was that of a man always perturbed when pertinent information wasn't already his.

I had neither energy nor inclination to go into it. "Later."

The helicopter's rotors whipped the air just outside.

"I have to go. My ride's here."

"Just when do you expect you'll ..."

I rang off.

The chopper landed and Lt. Col. Chuab disembarked. His uniform was as neatly pressed as ever. His shoes were as mirror-shined. His hair went through the rotor-blade downdraft without budging.

Roxanne intercepted him on the tarmac. They talked briefly. He looked in my direction. He nodded. He and Roxanne headed over.

"Lt. Col. Chuab wants to talk to you briefly here. Whatever other questions may arise he's agreed to ask in Bangkok."

Chuab had nothing to say about death by dyeing. "I know you probably feel like crap ..." Off by one-million percent! "... but we want to follow-up on that photo offer by Kenneth Critzer."

"You think he talks something other than bullshit?"

"Oh, it's all still grade-A bullshit, all right, but if we can per-suade you to turn over money for the photo, we can nab the bastard for fraud. A pain in our ass will be off the streets. We'll supply you with the money and with back-up. You just have to walk through it and walk away."

"He said if he spotted you and your friends, he'd bolt."

"Critzer isn't half as clever as he thinks. I'll get back to you with specifics, okay?"

"Sure."

Like a seeing-eye dog, Roxanne led me to the chopper. Like a mother hen, she tucked me into my seat and fastened my seatbelt.

"I'll talk to you soon," she said.

She kissed her fingertips and gently pressed them to my lips.

Then she exited, bent low beneath the whip-whip-whip of the rotors.

I hadn't told her about Jeff's call. Or, had I? If I hadn't, did she already know because the phone was bugged?

○ ○ ○

Back at the house on Litchi Klong, I informed the servants that I was headed directly to bed.

My room was blessedly dark.

I leaned my exhausted body against the shut door, my eyes closed.

I was tired, but I felt better. I felt so much better I started feeling guilty for not feeling worse.

I wouldn't have bothered with the lights, but I wanted (needed) a shower. The sudden illumination revealed two people on the bed. Thank God, both—a man and a woman—were alive! Thank God, too, they both were fully clothed! Strangely, they both looked familiar.

They were Thai. They were attractive. They remained seemingly non-threatening.

"You're in the wrong house?"

To which I got no response.

"You're in the wrong room?"

Still nothing.

"You're in the wrong universe?"

"Sammy sent us," the young man finally said. It was something an actor would say in a dated B-movie to gain entrance to some sleazy speakeasy. "Sammy Ped Mai."

So much for house security. Obviously, I could as easily be murdered in my Bangkok bed as die in a high-dive into a dyeing vat.

"Why did Sammy send you?"

"He wasn't sure if you like boys or girls," the young man explained but didn't answer my question. "Or, if you like both."

The guy was cute. He was thin. Maybe, he was too thin; or, maybe his muscles were just extra long and lean.

"Sammy sent you to ask my sexual preference?" This was getting more absurd by the moment.

"He said he owes you."

Roxanne had said she owed me. Now, Sammy Ped Mai said he owed me. Would I be any better off if and when I called in my markers?

"Sammy Ped Mai doesn't owe me," I said.

"He owes you because you found his grandmother," the young woman said.

She was a pretty little thing. She was doll-like in her big-bust, wasp-waist, Asian Barbie-doll sort of way. Jesus, Jesus, my cock was getting hard.

"I didn't find Sammy's grandmother," I said. "I found someone who pretended to be Sammy's grandmother. How does Sammy know I'd located anyone?"

"He just said you found her," the young woman said, confused. "He said you found her earlier today ... somewhere north of here ... in a house owned by Roxanne Whyte."

"No." I shook my head in emphasis. "It was a charade. It was a Nana doppelganger."

All of which flew over their heads like ducks over two very dry ponds.

"Sammy talked to a farmer," the young man said. "The farmer said, 'Yes, Emily Trang is here. Yes, the house she stays in belongs to Roxanne Whyte.'"

Stupid, stupid Sammy!

"Sammy said, 'Go to Mr. Draqual and thank him,'" the young woman said.

"Sammy will soon realize his mistake," I said. "Get him on the phone. I'll talk to him."

"He's not in Bangkok," the young man said. "He's up north."

"There must be some way to reach him."

The young man and the young woman simultaneously shrugged.

"Jesus!" I said. "Who's in charge at the knock-shop?"

More ducks flew over another dry pool.

"When Sammy isn't in Bangkok, like now, to whom do you report?" I tried again.

"Mildred Landruk," said the young woman.

"Portland Kijan," said the young man.

"Fuck!" said Stud Draqual and picked a name from the two offered. "Call Portland Kijan."

The young man looked doubtful.

"Yes, call him," I said. "Call him now. I want him to tell Sammy the woman in question is not his grandmother."

The young man looked more doubtful.

"Aren't you supposed to be here to do what I want?" I tried to put it in a way both might better understand.

I handed over the phone. The call proved long and loud. Then I asked for the receiver. Portland Kijan spoke not a word of decipherable English. I handed the phone back to the young man.

"Try to explain it to him one more time, please," I said.

He tried again. The conversation was so long I would have fallen asleep if it hadn't been so loud. Finally, the young man hung up.

I recognized him—suddenly—from the big-cock photo in Sammy's picture portfolio. The young woman was the one naked and sprawled seductively on ...

There was enough sexuality between them to re-grow the balls of a castrato, and all tired old me could think of to say was, "Where'd your photographer get those hot-pink sheets?"

The "Duh?", unsaid, was evident in their shared baffled expression.

"Come on, you two. Up and out. I've had a very exhausting day."

Surprisingly, I got no more argument. They merely exchanged glances and got up. The enormous bulge in Ram's pants was obscene.

After I put them out the front door, I took a long shower. I played silk larvae in hot-water cocoon. I folded my world in, then tried, ever so slowly, to unwind. I only touched my cock to wash it.

I dried my body with a towel warmed by a heat-rack. I slipped on a thick white robe either bought or stolen from The Oriental Hotel.

The previously dismissed young man—Ram, no forgetting that!—stood inside the bedroom.

"You're back." I wearily stated the obvious.

His smile put a deep dimple in each cheek. "Sammy said, 'If he sends you both away, it may just mean he's reluctant to have a woman hear him say he wants you. Go back and make sure.'"

"One more time: I didn't find Sammy's grandmother."

Ram shrugged. He only knew what he'd been told to do. He

only knew how to do it. A perfect sexual robot. With an exceptionally big cock, if ... With the possibilities of computer imaging these
days, there's no telling the true size of any dick in a picture.

"I'm really tired," I said. "I don't know how to put it any
more plainly."

"What about that?" He pointed to the bulge my hard cock
made in my robe.

Poor Ram! Like so many before him, he mistook spontaneous
erection for arousal.

"It doesn't mean anything, buddy," I said. "It happens all the
time. I haven't the energy to put it to any use, even if I wanted to."

Did I want to?

"Okay," he said, "how about you watch me go solo?" His dim-
ples deepened.

Afterwards, I'd blame my blatant voyeurism on my confusion in
having committed manslaughter. Or, I'd blame it on Ram, who was so
unable to understand the meaning of the simple little word, "No!"

In the morning, I offered to pay. Ram refused. Sammy had insisted
"whatever" was on the house. I gave Ram detailed instructions:
Sammy should contact me as soon as he was back in Bangkok and
understood that I'd not led him to his Nana. I'd see Ram got his
usual fee, plus tip. It was no fault of his if Sammy jumped the gun.

I walked Ram to the door of the bedroom.

My hand was on the doorknob when he brought up the subject
I had wanted to bring up all the previous evening (when Ram was-
n't performing and/or when I didn't watch or sleep): "It's okay to
ask if I knew Rhee Dulouk. Everyone wants to know, these days."

As if every cocksucker in Bangkok knew every other.

"I didn't know him," Ram said. That was that. "It was before I
came to work for Sammy that he and Rhee had their big fight."

Now that was interesting.

Did the police know? Did Jeff know? Did Stud Draqual, silk lingerie designer on a business trip in Thailand, want to know?

"Rhee pulled out on Sammy and went off on his own," Ram said and stepped in really close. He'd taken a shower, but his raw sexuality wasn't subjugated by mere soap and water. If he stepped any closer, the swell of his cock, halfway down his left leg, would touch my thigh.

"Rhee had Sammy shitting bricks and ready to build a house around him," he said. "Not that it should have come as any big surprise to Sammy that Rhee slept around and didn't give the boss a cut. Everyone but Sammy knew." His tongue slicked his lips.

"Rhee serviced some of Sammy's pretty important clients, but he stopped when he went out on his own. Sammy had to scramble for a replacement. Which left Sammy's clients furious. There was this one john who worked guard-duty at that new museum. Now, he was really upset. Hey, you know Miss Whyte of the museum, don't you? Great thing she and her uncle do to give back all that stuff to Thailand. Really great! They certainly didn't have to return any of it, did they? The way I hear it, no one around here knew just how much of Thailand Powell Whyte had in Los Angeles. And probably it still would be there if Miss Whyte had contested the will after her uncle died? So ..."

How did I pull him back on track? Did I try subtlety, or ... would subtlety be lost on Ram?

"This john, you say he worked guard-duty at the museum?"

"I can't remember his name, though we all knew it at the time. He screamed and shouted at Sammy when Rhee left. Sammy chewed nails and bitched up a storm for days afterwards."

I nodded to encourage the monologue.

"This guy never actually sounded as if he wanted Rhee back. He just sounded as if he didn't want him with anyone else. I've always figured he's the killer. Why else did he drop out of sight?"

Ram leaned in closer, providing the long-imagined press of his stiff dick. "How about I give you a little something before I go?"

"No stretch of the imagination, even mine, calls that cock of yours little."

He laughed.

"You'd just say no—again—if I offered you that," he said. "No, I want you to have this."

It was a stiletto with a triangular blade of medieval design. Any puncture wound from it wouldn't easily heal, would easily become infected, could be painfully fatal over a long period of time.

"Did you have that with you all night?" I sounded as if I actually thought it had been hocus-pocused out of thin air: this exquisite weapon, all shiny steel and ivory-cream handle.

"I never know when I might have to fight off unwanted advances. Although, I certainly didn't need to fight any off last night, did I?"

"I can't take your knife," I said. "You may need it. It looks valuable."

"I have others," he said. "It gives me pleasure to give you this one. The word on the street is that you need all the protection you can get."

"What else is said, on the street?"

"You should be careful. I wouldn't want anything to happen to you before I get in your pants."

It was harder and harder for me to blush in the face of such a constant onslaught of come-ons—from Jeff, from Roxanne, now from Ram.

None-too-subtlely, he dog-fucked his dick up against my leg. His breath smelled of peppermint. (Had he used my toothbrush and toothpaste?).

"I wouldn't want anything to happen to you before you get in my pants," he panted; it was but another variation on the same theme.

I accepted the knife. I collect them and I wanted that one as a souvenir.

He kissed me gently—flutter-of-a-butterfly-wing—on my cheek. For the second time in twelve hours, I accompanied him to the front door and closed it after him.

The Rhee Dulouk / Sammy Ped Mai connection was more grist for the mill. And meant what? Anything? Did I really care? What did the death of one young Thai prostitute matter to me? Was the newly gleaned information a ball to be tossed into Jeff's court?

I showered away the night's sweat, dressed, and went outside to the garden, where I lazed away the rest of the morning and the beginning of the afternoon.

"Yes, Damnern?" I'd made it a project to learn the servants' names, in order to list them for the police should someone more dangerous than Ram enter and exit the premises with immunity.

The houseboy's expression was ... wide-eyed? awe-struck? "You've a visitor."

So, was this visitor in the house? The house was cool, but I still savored the outside heat too much to be easily coaxed from it.

"Show him out here." I used a generic "him". If "he" were afraid of skin cancer, he could sit in the shade.

"You might prefer him at the front door."

"The front door?"

"If you would, Sir?" he insisted.

I stood, and went to greet my mysterious guest at the door.

Yikes!

Think Gainsborough's "The Blue Boy" gone horribly wrong and come to life on your stoop: lace ruffle at his neck; short, tight-fit wrinkly silk button-down-the-front jacket and tight-fit wrinkly silk high-water pants. Think pale blue hose. Think shoes with little azure bows. Wonder where in the hell is the flamboyant hat with its ostrich plume?

Think cerulean blue eye shadow and sapphire eyeliner. Think azure-tinted contact lenses (over dilated pupils). Think lip gloss so cobalt as to make the mouth appear flash-frozen.

Think vintage World War II motorcycle-with-sidecar, which stood incongruously in the background.

"Oh, Mr. Draqual, how wondrous it is to see you again!" proclaimed Sammy Ped Mai. "It makes my day stupendous!"

I wondered what the neighbors thought of this bizarre figure and what tales they would tell when the generous Cecil and his lovely wife returned.

Was Sammy there to collect for my untoward use of Ram's time and services? Guess again!

"I yearn so very much to 'play mother'," he said cryptically.

It seemed more likely he expected me to play mother.

"I insist you come to tea," he said.

"Tea?" I repeated. Some inner clock told me it was close to four in the afternoon, but my still-broken and unavailable wristwatch couldn't confirm it.

"My spies tell me that your Miss Whyte is presently occupied.

They also tell me that your Mr. Billing is presently ... well ... incognito. They tell me that you are presently here alone and neglected. I've come to your rescue."

"Tea?" I repeated for the second time: two down, and I'd probably make it three before my mind unlocked for normal conversation. My right hand physically cupped and pushed my jaw shut before it banged my shins.

"I'm really not dressed for tea, Sammy." My slacks and black form-fitting T-shirt didn't seem appropriate for a date with the Mad Hatter.

"All you need is a sports coat, dear boy."

"Dear boy": more a way for me to address him. He'd probably be as flattered as he imagined I was.

"How about you slip into one of your delicious Draqualian silks?"

He wanted me in ladies' lingerie?

"I only brought the one suit, Sammy, and it was ruined in the hotel explosion."

"Explosion. Ammunition. Would-be assassin dye-died. Such an adventuresome life you lead!"

"All of which leaves me in need of rest and recuperation," I said, trying a diplomatic cop-out.

"Exactly! What can be more restful and more recuperative than tea?"

"Sammy, I really do ..."

"I have some little adventures of my very own to impart over tea and biscuits," he interrupted. "They're not nearly as swashbuckling as yours, but they are interesting in that they expound upon how you saved me from some rat infested oubliette. Tit ..." He paused, as if uncertain anything to do with the female anatomy was really the appropriate word he was after. "... for tat making me want to reciprocate your surprising and unexpected largesse."

"I ... saved ... you ... from ... some ...?"

"So, hurry, hurry, and rescue whatever suitably fashion-frock accoutrement is incarcerated in your closet."

I needed a Thesaurus.

Did I stay? Did I go? Did I invite him in? Would Cecil and his wife come up minus a few expensive knickknacks if I let this Thai blue-boy pass from front door to garden?

"I should hate to have to throw a conniption," Sammy added.

If I decided to go with him ... God, please, nowhere public! Did I dare leave him peacock-like on the doorstep while I went to rescue the frock accoutrement incarcerated in my closet?

"Love your Gucci loafers, by the way" he said. "I'll bet you'd look stunning in full leather drag. Why don't I wait in our conveyance while you get jacketed?"

He did a rather spiffy about-face and proceeded to the vintage World War II motorcycle with sidecar.

I went inside and shut the door behind me.

Damnern was across the room, his look one of complete ...

"I'm going out for a while," I said.

... abject disbelief? ... utter chagrin? ... sheer horror? ... "Oh, Sir, you're out of your fucking mind!"?

"If Miss Whyte calls, tell her I'm not sure when I'll be back."

No need for me to add, "I'm off with Sammy Ped Mai." The man-boy's flaunting had the advantage of pointing an accusing finger right in his direction should anything happen to me. Otherwise, I would have been more concerned. After all, Madam Elephant, according to Lt. Col. Chuab, had her fingers in prostitution (Sammy's bailiwick), as well as in gun-running and, more importantly, gun-for-hire assassinations.

Damnern looked downright discombobulated when I headed out the door.

I expected to play chauffeur to Sammy who, full of surprises, straddled the seat of the motorcycle like a kid perched atop his very first bicycle, complete with training wheels.

"You look genuinely fetching!" he proclaimed loud enough for all of Bangkok to hear. "Don't I wish I could wear clothes like you do."

He might start by shopping somewhere other than a costume-supply shop.

"Embark! Embark!" he insisted.

The sidecar was all mine. I wasn't all in it, nor all ready for departure, when he had the cycle started, in gear, and racing out the driveway.

There was too much noise for articulate conversation. Good thing, because it took all of my concentration to keep my head down (God, let me be invisible!), and hold on while Sammy took us on one helluva ride. Not since my last James Bond movie had I seen so many hapless pedestrians run so fast to get out of the way.

I began to remember the pleasure I once took in my Harley Hog. The Harley was discarded, when? It was long before the polo accident and my doctor's orders of, "No more!" It was even before my plunge into white-water rafting and into white-water.

"Wheeeee!" squealed Sammy and took us into a corner that put every county-fair whirligig ride to shame. I pressed hard against one side of the sidecar; the other side levitated. His abrupt stop threw me forward and left me disoriented and confronting an absolutely charming house. Although in miniature, it wasn't entirely scaled to dollhouse proportions. It stood on low stilts, with slanted walls, steeply slanted thatch roof, decorative kalae, gables with ngaos, and window pediments. Constructed entirely of hardwoods and bamboos, the building was couched within intimate and insulating greenery that struck me as recently miniature bonsai gone suddenly into larger-growth rebellion. Best described as private Strickette, as opposed to public, this small architectural masterpiece, if belonging to Sammy, meant ...

"There must be a lot of money in purveying."

"Ah, yes," he said. "In purveying and in ... other things."

His purposeful pause insinuated: Gun-running. Organized crime. Blackmail. Prostitution.

"Stocks and bonds," he said. Which insinuated: Gun-running. Organized crime. Blackmail. Prostitution.

"It's all ..." I nodded toward the house and environs. " ... genuinely quite charming."

"More so, for me, when it was new," he said. Then, he sighed. "How quickly we become jaded."

I had the distinct impression he would like to include me in the "we".

Just how jaded Sammy had become was evident, once inside, by how blasély he bypassed the truly exquisite tiny Thai furnishings in favor of an interior room, the latter's door shut behind us.

"This room ..." His all-encompassing wave of both arms was so grandiose he almost fell over. "... is how I imagine England. Unfortunately, I've never been there."

It was a Victorian clutter of chairs, sofas, tables, and tablecloths (that drooled to puddles on the rugs), picture frames, peacock feathers, a stuffed weasel (?), and heavy drapery. A highly polished silver tea service was set on a highly polished silver tray on a linen-water-falled low table accompanied by a cart of myriad crustless heart-, spade-, diamond-, club-cut sandwiches and scrumptious desserts, between two couching chairs.

"Please, please," he limp-wristed me toward one chair convenient to the tea service.

To get there, I felt like Theseus out to maneuver the Cretan maze. Sammy finally got to "play mother" and poured tea into delicate see-through bone-China cups on delicate see-through bone-China saucers.

"This blend is a particular favorite of mine," he said. "It's a pinch of congou, a bit of oolong, a smidgen of bohea ..."

Its steam smelled lovely. I'd yet to see another soul, but someone had to have made things ready. The tea was good, made more so by an ever-so-slight squeeze of flavor-enhancing lemon.

Let's converse," he said.

"Okay." I was amiable, sequestered comfortably, as we were, away from a gawking public.

"Gratitudes are in order."

"I appreciate that you sent Ram and the young lady," I said.

"Oh, silly boy!" he waved me off before I could offer reimbursement for Ram's solo performance. "Not you thanking me. Vice versa."

"For what?"

His laugh as much as said silly-you. "Saving me from insidious machinations to ensnare me. Jail, I reiterate, would have been my fate."

He mistook my misunderstanding for modesty.

"Come now, dear, dear boy. You're owed. Of course, you are. I would have gone barging right in. And not even my Nana there to greet me. Instead policemen—repeat: the cops!—to be sure. Accusations. Breaking-and-entering charges. Robbery charges. Maybe the old girl with a bruise or two; blame it on me. Assault. Someone—though not I, I assure you—produces a gun. Assault with a deadly weapon charges. So many are ready to believe me capable of any and all. Even those gracious enough to think, 'So, just maybe, he's innocent, this time?' could easily be persuaded and figure, 'Oh hell, he was guilty so many times and walked, send him down the tube, up the river, good-bye, so-long, been good to know you, have a good time, and throw away the key, hallelujah, hosanna, in Excelsus Deus.'" He took a large and audible breath. "I was saved by your insistence that Ram pick up the telephone and apprise me of the circumstances.

"Ram's impressed. Ram is hardly ever impressed. Certainly never by people. Thinks the worst of them, most every time. Has, I guess, seen them at their worst. Over a far longer time than you might imagine. Ram far more antique than most believe. So few people notice his real age, distracted by that behemoth dangling so ponderously between his solar plexus and knees."

Sammy sounded—sans cock talk—much like Roxanne trying to out Sammy as Methuselah in clever disguise.

"I should have his genes," Sammy said, covetously. "I should have his velvety skin and girlish complexion."

"Hell, then, I should have his cock," I said and, of course, meant literally attached to my lower belly, its bulge my bulge. But Sammy misinterpreted.

"You could have had it, the way I hear it," he said. "In the ass, down the throat, in the fist. Rubbed to climax between your thighs. Only you just wanted to watch what Ram could do with it. A waste, to my way of thinking, to Ram's way of thinking. But now we've a better notion, things can progress faster."

"Things?"

"Let's wait and see," said Sammy and smiled over the rim of see-through bone-China. His blue eyeliner threatened to run in the steam of special blend.

"I was surprised when I heard you thought Roxanne took me to your grandmother." I wanted him back on track.

"Miss Whyte is so very clever. Knew I knew she'd absconded with Nana. Perused me like a tome. She knew I'd have her followed. She knew I'd make assumptions. She knew I'd show up and .... well ..."

Gently I placed my empty teacup on its saucer; gently Sammy poured more tea.

"Why did you call and tell me, I wonder?" Sammy said. Slyness accompanied the curiosity so obvious in his voice and in his stare.

If you've a choice between telling the truth or telling a lie, and the truth works, always tell the truth. "The woman wasn't your Nana. I didn't feel it fair that you might be lead to think she was."

A boy/man used to clandestine stratagem (how about "those"

words, Sammy?) could not help but look for clandestine stratagem.

"So, you deemed it fortuitous to chock up favor-owed?" he asked. "So you saw me well-placed to help succor your very attractive ass?" He made it sound downright obscene.

"Beg your pardon?"

He laughed. Giggled, really. He drank more tea in punctuation.

"You shot at. Nearly blown up. Damn near dumped to die in dye. Rumor goes your name finds itself on the hit list of the elusive Madam Elephant. With all that, maybe you figure a friend, entrenched within Thailand's underbelly, will prove more useful than Miss Whyte, at least in this regard?"

"Madam Elephant has me on her hit list?" Inquiring mind wanted to know.

"How's a mere purveyor to know the craniums of his betters? I do hear Madam Elephant had a chance, up-close personal, to kill you, more recent than your die-dye-job experience. Your demise on-the-verge. Madam Elephant having you almost on death's doorstep. But, you still live. Handsome as ever. You've not lost one finger or toe. Nor, I assume, have you been dispossessed of your cock or even one testicle."

As if blood stains had been missed, he focused on my crotch. Fortunately, table and tea set were in the way.

"Do you know Madam Elephant's real name?" I came right on out and asked him.

His hands raised to head level, palms outward, and pushed air towards me. "Oh, my dear boy, any favor-owed certainly doesn't cover the cost of that! Even if I knew. It's hard to imagine that you really want to know. The price of knowing is often so exorbitant, even for those with need-to-know." With one quick movement, he sawed the edge of his open hand lengthwise across his neck. "Yours such a handsome throat. It has potential, an A-one cocksucker's throat, according to Ram."

I shuddered to my Gucci loafers with the thought of Ram's ram throat-rammed.

"Ram's 'the' authority on cock-sucking, ass-fucking, self-fellatio, anything, each and everything that's male-male sexual. Wants to do more for and to you than you've allowed. Did I say he thinks you the handsomest? Thinks you fascinating? 'Fascinating,' his exact word."

"Right!" I knew bullshit (but to what purpose?) when I heard it.

"Where are my manners?" he said and reached for one of the pastries on the adjoining cart. "Wrap your sexy oral orifice around this delectable cream-filled morsel." With these words, he took one himself, bit down with the eager abandon of a child, and drooled creamy contents over his lips, his chin, and his fingers.

Texes (with its second "e") Bob's is a disco/bar/nightclub on Patpong 1, between Silam and Surawang Roads, Bangkok. Its possible misspelling insinuates a less-than-English-adept Thai, intend upon capitalizing on the looking-for-a-home-away-from-home sensibilities of American GIs who so often R&R'd in Thailand, during the Vietnam War. Except, the place has been where it is, name unchanged, since the fifties. No one I've ever met has a clue as to whether there ever was a character, Texas (or Texes) Bob, and/or if the mistake occurred in the sign shop where English-ignorant workers bent neon tubes into the twisted red-flashing script that invites neophytes and long-time converts to sample one of the city's more famous flesh-pots.

The place is reached by walking, or driving, a gauntlet of nightlife that, like partial menus, entices with hints of full-course meals.

Male and female mud wrestlers indulge pig-pen style. Kick boxers kick: one another or solo; Kung-fu movies put to shame. Real women (or he/she drags), cajole reluctant (sometimes not) customers into always dark bars where they're enticed to buy always expensive drinks. The area is renown for King's Castle, Queen's Castle, and the Mississippi Club (where scenes of "The Deer Hunter" were filmed).

I'd been to Texes Bob's before. Is there anyone who has visited Bangkok and hasn't been there? I'd gone with friends. The theory had been that there is protection in numbers. No one was likely to stray far with someone along to tell the tale of tail.

I felt increasingly uneasy going there with Sammy Ped Mai. I was made even more so by my quickly acquired suspicions that Sammy may well own a part-interest in the establishment. I hadn't seen so much deference, bowing-low, and ass-kissing, since England's Prince Philip made his entrance after the polo match his team played (and lost) against mine in Miami Beach.

Sammy stepping into the place was like seeing the members of an orchestra brought up short by a master conductor's imperceptible (except to them) slight-of-baton. Everyone went literally dead-stop and turned in Sammy's direction.

I might have thought it was because he'd changed into a tight-fitting little-boy sailor suit (reminiscent of those pictures of Alexis, son of Tsar Nicholas) complete with bell-bottoms and little sailor's hat, but there was already too much bizarrerie (Yo, Sammy!) in the room to make Sammy stand out. One young man wore nothing but a thong and a dog-collar, the latter attached by a leash to his similarly clothed and collared companion. Another young man wore cowboy chaps, bikini briefs, a cowboy hat. There were almost too many transvestites to mention (some obvious, some not quite so obvious).

A brief nod from Sammy, an even more brief limp-wrist wave from him, and all went back to normal (or, rather, back to not-so-normal).

"I really don't know if ..." I began protest for not the first time. He'd said he would ride along while his driver dropped me off at the house on Litchi Klong. He'd never mentioned it would be the long way home, with an interim pit stop.

"Too cacophonous to hear you, my boy," Sammy interrupted. "This way."

The crowd parted, like the Red Sea for Moses. It closed, as quickly, pharaoh's men just as likely to have died in this onrush.

I thought we headed for the one empty table, guarded by flanking human giants. Instead, we skirted the table and passed through a door I didn't know was even there until it shut behind us.

"Ah," said Sammy within the gloom and comparative silence of the hidden hallway, "the pandemonium was nearly unbearable, was it not?"

"Indubitably," I said.

"Indubitably," he echoed. His mouth dexterously loved the word as a pig savored a newly snouted-out truffle.

I was afraid he'd ask for a definition. I had none, except for context which once had a fashion critic flatter me, and call my competition's Spring collection, "Indubitably horrific!" Sammy, though, like I had, accepted the word because it "seemed" to fit.

"This way," he said and headed to the right.

"Sammy, I ..." I was Theseus who questioned the veracity of the thread provided by Ariadne.

"We'll talk, dear boy," he called back over one shoulder. "For now, follow along."

I contemplated bolting. God only knew where he took me. A glance back provided no clue as to how or where the now-invisible door accessed the nightclub. Like a vulnerable lion cub that followed the white spots on the backs of its mother's ears, I followed the wiggle of Sammy's buttocks-in-white bell-bottom trousers. I couldn't believe the maze that existed and which we maneuvered. I couldn't believe the sounds I heard, some from behind closed doors, some from cubbyholes with doors wide open. The latter, also, provided live pornographic visuals made more titillating by my side-show-hasty glimpses made in passing.

I saw a strobe-lit woman sandwiched between two cock-stabbing men, and Sammy-as-Ariadne metamorphosed into Sammy-as-Beatrice; I-as-Theseus metamorphosed into I-as-Dante; back-bar labyrinth metamorphosed into hellish maze from the Inferno.

"Sammy, I really must insist ..."

He disappeared.

I experienced a sudden abandoned-in-Hades helplessness that washed through me.

With no beacon-wiggling-ass to follow, I was adrift and slowed almost to a stop when I was literally manhandled sideways. My swift exit of the hallway was punctuated by the thud of the door between it and me.

I expected more than just Sammy and I, but we were the only two in the room. He moved behind a paper-cluttered desk but didn't sit. Mounted on the wall behind him was an exquisitely carved elephant tusk whose multi-layer bas-reliefs of mermaid, fish, flute, and intricate seascapes, depicted scenes from Sunthorn Phu's epic poem "Phra Aphaimani".

Sammy motioned me toward one of the only two available chairs. I, like he, didn't sit.

"I should get back, Sammy. Really."

"Could ... would ... should." He waved his arm in airy dismissal, like cow tail dispersed irritating flies. "There's time enough for you to get back home, my boy."

He smiled and not very pleasantly.

"It's safer for you here, I would expect," he said. "Here, not likely anything untoward happens without my precognition."

Why didn't I find that in the least bit comforting?

"You've yourself in a rut, dear boy," he said. "Where's the excitement once had? Polo? Mountain-climbing? Where's white-water rafting?"

He'd done his homework.

"All replaced by bullets, bombs, and assassins out to dye me green," I said.

"The difference, my dear boy ..." He put both hands on the desktop and leaned toward me. "... is the latter came looking for you, the former you searched out."

"Actually, I had a polo accident."

"Ah, 'the' polo accident," said Sammy, in indication that this part of my story hadn't escaped him. "Left you impotent, did it?"

"Christ, no!"

Was he the only one on the face of the Earth who couldn't see my boner and comment upon it?

"Confirmed by the bulge in your pants."

He wasn't blind after all.

"So, we must assume that your polo accident performed some other trick on your libido. Somehow shifted certain gears. Accounting for your lessening of interest in women." (Something Dr. Melissa insinuates hadn't needed lessening). "Possibly even less-ening your interest in men." (Something Dr. Melissa insinuates is definitely not the case). "Which possibly opened you more fully to the possibilities of voyeurism." (God and Dr. Melissa only knew where she signed off on that one).

Little else, I suppose, Sammy could have deduced after my Night Watch (Rembrandt material?) with Ram-of-the-big-ram?!

He did a smooth pirouette and faced the file cabinet behind him. The folder he chose was already pulled and on top of the cab-inet. It was so much of an armful, his pirouette in return wasn't nearly as graceful as the one that preceded. He dropped the folder, the plop of which would have squashed any insect. Desk papers shifted outward from point of contact; one sheet of paper, ignored, fluttered to the floor.

The pregnant folder birthed a landslide of photographs. The top one would have made good evidence in the defense of Robert Maplethorpe's photography as art not porn; this billy-club-AND-bullwhip-handle-up-naked-young-man's-ass definitely was the latter.

"We have multitudinous live-show-presentation possibilities, from the truly mundane to truly sublime. They're all available for your viewing delectation."

"Have you heard the one about how it's a mistake to assume, in that it makes an 'ass' out of 'u' and 'me'?"

"No," he said. His eyes and voice were riddled with glee. "Ass-u-me! Wonderful!"

Actually, it was more along the lines of older-than-the-hills.

"Certainly that will be plagiarized by me, no credit given to you," he said.

"It might be best if you took the thought to heart, as far as my being here," I said.

"You didn't like watching Ram?"

How did I finesse my way out of and/or around that one?

"I was tired, and ..."

"Ah, no! Please, no! Not from you, my dear boy. I expect so much more than the hackneyed, 'I was tired.' 'I was drunk!' 'I was drugged.'"

(Did Dr. Melissa look for a soul mate?)

"This is Sammy Ped Mai, Stud. Seen it all, and I mean all. Capital 'A'; capital 'double toothpicks'. What's a little voyeurism to me? Nothing! Actually, it comes off disgustingly normal, in that I would wish you were downright degenerate. What a good time I could show you then!"

He Pontius-Pilate washed his waterless soap-free hands with air.

"I do want to show you a good time, because I like you ... because I owe you. I did mention I want to do this free? Gratis? On the house? No remuneration necessary or required? Or ..."

His eyes went squinty. His dilated pupils became hardly visible through narrowed slits. It wasn't something he would do if he saw himself in the mirror, because it caused every fine line at the outside of his eyes to assume major-rut status.

"... Miss Whyte possibly insinuates nothing is free, as far as Sammy Ped Mai is concerned. You know everything she says about me is biased by her dislike of me? And, what have I ever done to her?"

I was grateful for the opportunity to veer the conversation from the sexual. "Roxanne takes extreme offense to you having hit your Nana."

"Oh, so, it's a fucking woman thing!" he said in obvious exasperation.

I would have begged to differ. Hitting a woman, let alone one's own old granny, was something I, as well as Roxanne, found personally repellent. Did I tell him that, though? Call me chicken (although, I've played polo, rafted dangerous waters, climbed seemingly impossible peaks, with the very best), but no way I bearded this particular lion in his own den.

"Well, maybe it's not 'just' a woman thing," Sammy conceded in afterthought. "It's an Occidental thing, as well. It's an inherent inability of the Western mind-set to shed its own perspectives and come at things the way those things play in their countries of origin. My grandmother caused me to lose face. Something you, too, cause me if you don't let me begin repayment for service rendered. Didn't your mother ever tell you that when offered a gift merely say, 'Yes, please', and 'Thank-you'?"

"Thai tradition allows you to sock your poor old granny?"

"She's an ingrate and no longer a 'poor' one, either."

He sat down.

I sat down.

He screwed up his mouth to show even more wrinkles. "I supported the old harridan for years and years and years. Kept her alive when I, myself, was barely able to subsist. I did so, because she's blood. I'm her only family. It was my duty. As it is her duty, now, suddenly into a good deal of money, to do other than try to cut me off completely. After all, I'm not out to bilk her out of her money. No! I want merely to manage it for her, as I've managed my own money ... as I've always managed higher returns of interest than what's offered by banks, by stocks, or by bonds."

I didn't (repeat: did not) remind him of his earlier inference that stocks and bonds had helped provide him his exquisitely crafted house.

"My Nana's money has the definite advantage of ..."

He stopped, as if he may have recognized his diarrhea of the mouth. He'd already said enough for me to infer his granny's money, because it was legitimate, had no special need for "laundering". There were all sorts of possibilities for her legal money to be used illegally, via clever financial manipulations, to make it the "soap" that would see companion dirty money seem perfectly clean.

"Roxanne tells you I lure businessmen and politicians here, lower their inhibitions, turn loose their sexual fantasies, photograph and blackmail them afterwards?"

Even the notion of such activities was enough to take a bit of the starch out of my pecker.

"I've a politician in one of these very rooms, right now. Never here before but here now. Because he knows Sammy Ped Mai doesn't hoodwink friends. But, since you probably don't yet consider me a friend, although I hope you remain open-minded to that possibility, I can guarantee you that Sammy Ped Mai doesn't hoodwink the people he likes. And, we like you."

Beware of people, unless real queens, who refer to themselves in first-person plural: a Draqualism.

"Common sense tells you ... should tell you ... must tell you ... that to hoodwink a few politicians is easy. I can't begin to tell you how easy. All I need do is put them into a room with a naked boy, a naked girl, a donkey, and they can't control themselves, no matter how many pictures I snap. But politicians who get an office can lose it. They come, they go. What use are they after they're gone? What damage is done to my reputation if word gets out to the newly 'in' that Sammy Ped Mai has blackmailed the recently 'out' and should be avoided at all cost?"

There was a knock on the door, and the door opened without permission-given. There was no "Mother-may-I?" And "mother" was livid. Sammy's brows furrowed. His face turned beet-red.

"What in the hell do you want, when I left explicit instructions I ... did ... NOT ... want ... to ... be ... disturbed?!"

The mist of his venom spat the desktop.

Have you ever seen really frightened? The young lady in the open doorway looked genuinely in fear for her life. She trembled like a drenched kitten in the rain, in the middle of the highway, in the dark, in the direct path of a sixteen-wheeler, free of monitoring "Smokies", that barreled down the pavement at a hundred-plus miles an hour. She was petite: less than five-feet. Thin-to-skinny, big black eyes, short black hair. She had too much makeup. She wore too few clothes: a brassiere, panties, a garter belt, stiletto heels.

"I was told ..." she said, and she came across as a helpless sparrow that sang for succor in blustery hurricane winds.

"Told? Told!"

Sammy's sudden revelation ... epiphany ... whispered secretly to him from on-high could be literally seen in his change of demeanor. If he wasn't exactly a lion converted to a pussy cat, conversion of lion to fox did come to mind. His tone of voice, though, remained less affected.

"Here," he said roughly. He pointed to his left ear. "From your rosebud labia to my auricle."

Did he know the cunt-to-heart-atrium picture he painted?

She smelled of potent eau de toilette: a hardly subtle miasma of gardenia and carnation and lilac. It made me lethargic as she walked it around me to Sammy behind the desk. She whispered in his ear.

He watched me watch him and left his expression deadlocked.

"Fine," he said to her whispered couple of words. "Sure. Okay. Why not? Of course. Right-O."

The young woman scuttled (no other way to describe her agitated crab-like retreat and exit).

"No shock, I suppose, that a man as good-looking as you should have so many people, bad and good, interested in him," he explained. "Quite aside from the fact that I, personally, find you so delicious, which frankly surprises me. Usually, Occidental men are so pale and pasty, I find it's rather like bedding whitefish or dissanguinated zombies. That said ..."

There was a quick rap on the door, and the door opened. A woman—not the one so recently left—glided in. She had a long and lean model's body. Her fashionably open-toe shoes had medium-heels. Her long legs were encased within a pair of pale beige hose. Her stylishly plain-black silk slip-dress, with its spaghetti straps, masqueraded as Draqualian, but its silk was less expensive and less-luminescent and was as fake as the Gucci, Armani, and Versace stockpiled within the clutter of the roadside stalls outside. The woman's breasts weren't large, but any larger would have looked far less stylish in the dress she wore. Her neck, long and slender, was jewelry-free, as were her arms and fingers. Her face had the right amount of understated makeup: a pale foundation, a touch of blush to accentuate her cheekbones, a minimum of eyeliner and eye-shadow, a veneer of lip gloss to ...

"Jesus!" I couldn't help myself. My surprise was spontaneous and genuine. "Ram?"

Thailand's world of prostitution is full of drag queens. The notion, though, had never occurred to me that Ram, with his exceptionally large endowment, would/could ever be one of them. What skill and effort to contain Ram's extraordinary physical aberration into such a state of subjugation that it didn't provide the slightest bulge beneath the clinging material of his dress! His monster cock had to be bound and tied, tucked between his legs, anchored with cord or tape. Even the notion of its attempted erection, it presently so thoroughly caged a beast, made me ache in sympathy.

"Stud," he said and moved behind my chair, put his hands with perfectly manicured long (but not too-long) artificial nails, painted the same pale pink as his lips, to my shoulders. He bent over me, preceded by the light and airy smell of vanilla. He kissed the top of my head. "How nice to see you again."

Even his voice had changed. While still low, it was softer. It was no more obviously the voice of a man-pretending-to-be-woman than were his demeanor and clothes. He'd successfully escaped the pitfall of so many transvestites who went for overkill and ended up looking more woman than any real woman ... and were recognized as fake because of it.

He moved from behind me and whipped a vanilla-scented breeze. His wig was black human hair, medium cut, pulled back on one side and attached by one black ebony chopstick into a modified French roll. The other side hung loose in a well-coiffed parenthesis that frequently, coquettishly, draped its half of his face.

"Ah, Sammy presents viewing possibilities," he said when he reached the desk. Sammy shrugged, palms turned up. Ram selected the top photo—naked young man with billy club and whip handle—and said, "Ko Trat performs this amazing feat with far more stylish aplomb than this picture suggests." There was only the slightest dismissal in the moue of his incredibly sexy mouth. "Has it been decided, then, that something B&D/S&M is to your liking?"

"I was just telling Sammy I really don't have the time for anything this evening." Period!

"Good," Ram said, surprised. He let the photo flutter, of its own accord, to the desktop. "I'm otherwise occupied this evening, and I think you would particularly enjoy my leather-and-chains persona. I'm sure you'd derive a great deal of viewing pleasure and satisfaction were you to see me, manacled, take another leather man's big cock up my tight ass. You must insist Sammy make the arrangements."

He reached over and, with one pink-painted fingernail, touched Sammy's jawline and kept him focused. "I think we should call up one of those studly white boys from Embassy Row. Stud will likely find it more enjoyable if it's one of his fellow Caucasians on the delivering end of any cock up my butt."

"I ..." I'd protested all evening and could probably continue to do so until I was blue in the face without successfully making my point.

"Sammy will handle everything, won't you, Sammy?"

Ram backtracked within his deliciously enveloping vanilla fragrance. He stopped by me and smiled. "You really should close your mouth, Stud," he said. "While I find your wide-eyed look irrefutably erotic, hot and flattering, you might unwittingly catch a fly."

He laughed. It was low, soft, musical. Okay, it was sexy.

He provided another kiss to the crown of my head and a parting, "Can't wait!". Suddenly he was gone, the door closing softly behind him.

His essence of vanilla lingered, but it wasn't enough to keep my attention from Sammy, whose expression was for the first time truly inscrutable.

"Well, then," Sammy said. He gathered up the recalcitrant photo of the naked young man with billy club and whip handle. He replaced it with its companion pictures and reversed their waterfall to fit, albeit to overflowing, their original cover. "That does make things so much easier, doesn't it?" Was he being facetious?

"I do need to get back," I insisted.

"Do you want to go through my photos of exhibitionistic Caucasians available from Embassy Row or from regularly-to-Bangkok flight crews? Or, will you trust my judgement in providing someone who'll meet your and Ram's expectations, visually and otherwise?"

"I really must go." I was adamant about departure. I was non-committal about the "other".

He stood. I stood, relieved in that I'd finally made headway. Though I wasn't sorry I'd come. It had proved an interesting, even pleasant, peek at Bangkok's underbelly. I hadn't been required to dodge one bullet, bomb, or weapon-wielding madman.

Sammy picked up the bulky folder and returned it to its previous spot atop the file cabinet.

"Do you have a picture of everyone who works for you?" I asked his back.

"Such pictures are so convenient," he said and turned back in my direction. His sailor hat sat his head at a boyishly cocky angle. "A potential customer's tastes are so hard to determine cold, short of parading the whole coterie of available delectables."

"And if someone should leave your service, what happens to his photo?"

"If he or she leaves under favorable circumstances, I may keep it as a memento, or I may give it as a souvenir of happy times spent here. If he or she leaves under less-than-favorable circumstances, I call in a witch to use the photo in a curse-spell; the photo is burned, and its ashes are secreted in some convenient graveyard."

"Oh." Not exactly what Mr. Curiosity-At-Work wanted to hear.

"Oh?" he echoed me, only in question-form.

"I suppose your photo of Rhee Dulouk, by now, is long cursed, burned, and buried."

"Why would I have a photo of Rhee Dulouk?"

"You remember? That young Thai prostitute who ..."

"... in getting his throat cut sent one Mr. Billing into a vengeful rampage. Of course, I remember. Rhee worked for my competition."

Okay! Sammy didn't want to fess up to it, fine by me. I saw his point. As far as I knew, no one but Ram—not the police, nor Jeff—had made any Rhee Dulouk/Sammy Ped Mai connection.

"Who told you that Rhee Dulouk was one of mine?"

"The way I hear it, your final argument was loud and long enough for any number of people to have heard," I said, covering Ram's ass (figuratively speaking, of course).

"Ram told you, didn't he?"

I didn't comment.

"Sure he did. To whom else around here except to me, have you exhibited affable friendliness?"

"Whoever told me, I have no intentions of it going any farther," I said. Let Lt. Col. Chuab do his own footwork. As for telling Jeff ... I didn't dislike Sammy so much as to make his quiet purveyor's life unnecessarily complicated by Jeff .

"Thank-you. I would, yet again, be most gratefully indebted."

"Now, if you could show me the way out, I can take a taxi back to Litchi Klong."

He picked up the phone and, within seconds, one of the large men from the distant door was in attendance.

"See that Mr. Draqual gets back to where he's staying," Sammy said.

He gave a final nod of farewell, preoccupied enough to make me hope my big mouth hadn't gotten Ram in hot water.

17

I was running late when Damnern said I had a phone call. Still half-dressed, I checked my wrist for the watch that I'd not worn since the timepiece broke on the river. I answered the phone.

"I thought I'd wish you luck on this morning's little adventure," Jeff said from the other end of the line. "You did say it was this morning, didn't you? I'm positive Lt. Col. Chuab persuaded you to follow-through, right? You just need to make sure you use police money, not your own, in case Critzer successfully gives the cops the slip. Wouldn't be the first time."

"I'm about to head out, even as we speak."

"I thought I'd warn you how my contacts tell me the guy is a real piece of work. He may even be who and what he says he is. He may even have what he says he has. The police are possibly making it seem less a big deal, because they don't want to scare you away from bringing in Critzer and a much-wanted Madam Elephant I.D."

"Well, doesn't that just make my day!"

"Just make sure you take good care of that cute butt of yours.

Lt. Col. Chuab isn't nearly as fond of it as I am."

He rang off.

I taxied to a jeweler and bought a Concord watch. My life-style, more and more often these days, demanded a timepiece robust as well as fashionable. I was assured the watch was not only rugged but water-proof down to 99 feet.

I went to the bank and participated in the charade that it was my money being handed over in the metal briefcase in case Critzer or one of his minions watched.

I took a cab to Rajadamri Road and had the driver park across from the Royal Bangkok Sport Club Race Track. Two long blocks ahead, hardly visible, was the Saladang Intersection, where Rajadamri Road met Rama IV Road and converted to Silon Road on the other side. I asked the driver to wait, opened the door, and stepped out. The maze of walkways, trees, and lakes that make up Lumpini Park, one of the few public oases of greenery in a city of over four-million people, loomed on my left. I noted someone lazily slept on the grass. Where the park formed its obtuse angle to mirror the Saladang Intersection, I stopped walking.

I waited.

I checked my new watch. Either it was already running fast, or Critzer was running slow. I checked for Lt. Col. Chuab or his back-up. Across the street, someone objected to the man sleeping in the park, shouting and pointing. The sleeping man slept on.

"Come on, Critzer. Come bloody on!"

A woman screamed, a blood-curdling scream that raised the hair along my arms. Suddenly, there were sirens ... flashing lights ... cops. Nice undercover work, boys!

With a screech, one cop car pulled up and stopped at the curb directly beside me. Lt. Col. Chuab, inside, was soon outside and motioning me in.

"What?"

"Just wait here," he said.

The door closed and locked. The driver baby-sat.

"What's going on?" I asked.

"Seems there's a dead body in the park."

"Critzer?"

The driver shrugged.

It was Critzer, all right, confirmed by Lt. Col. Chuab, who was back in the car within minutes.

"Is he dead from natural causes?"

"He's dead from some kind of sharp instrument. Probably multiple stab-wounds from a knife."

"Did you get the photograph?"

"It looks like Madam Elephant got to him and the photograph before we did. He's likely been a marked man since that gun deal went wrong."

"So now you concede Critzer just may have been involved in gun-running?" If that part of Critzer's tale was true, why not the rest of it, photo included?

"Critzer was involved in a lot of things. Most of which are still best not complicated by civilians. Take Mr. Draqual home," Lt. Col. Chuab told the driver, and exited the police car with the police money.

"Four-nine-six Litchi Klong Road," I instructed the driver. Amateur detective or not, I still find death scenes disturbing. As the car pulled away, I didn't even look back.

I would have stayed at the house sipping booze for the rest of the day if Roxanne hadn't called, told me "things" kept her from joining me for lunch, and suggested, a la Chuab, it might "be safer" if I stuck around the premises. I wasn't about to succumb to circumstances that kept me a prisoner even in such pleasant surroundings.

Roxanne's excuse for keeping me put was the expected call from Jeff. She wanted to get him word, ASAP, they could ideally meet the next afternoon. Whoever it was she'd waited for was apparently now available. I figured if Jeff wanted to contact me, he could as easily access the phone number of some local eatery as call the house on Litchi Klong. The former would likely provide less chance of electronic bugs.

I took a cab to a raan kuay teow whose noodles had been recommended by a friend shortly before I left New York. Kuay teow is a way of life in Thailand. Like the quest for the Holy Grail, there's an ongoing search for the perfect bowl of noodles. Fortunes are made by humble street vendors who suddenly become celebrated for their secret succulent broth. My last visit to Bangkok, the sen yai of one particular vendor had been the noodle of the hour, purported to have aphrodisiacal powers (this was later proven not to be the case, and the vendor was bankrupted).

Jeff surprised me by joining me, arm out of its sling, and looking far less haggard than when last I saw him. I couldn't imagine
how he knew I wasn't followed. However, he was professional
enough not to be where he was if it wasn't safe for him.

"Your arm," I referenced its apparent improvement.

"Almost as good as new," he said. He lifted it. He patted the hidden area of the wound, albeit gently. He and I ordered noodles.

"I heard about Critzer," he said. "Good riddance to bad rubbish
is the way I hear it."

"And his killer had the extremely good grace to do the deed
before I made my appearance," I said.

Jeff's noodles arrived. He fanned the steam incense-like in his
direction with the cupped palms of both hands: a regular noodle
gourmet. He tasted, with an audible slurp, as if testing the bouquet
of some fine wine.

"Not bad," he said. "I've wanted to try this place for ages."

"You're here for noodles, then, not because you're psychic?"

He looked at me over the rim of his steaming bowl. "I'm here,
because I like looking at you, and I get tired of just imagining how
you look over some lousy phone."

"The reason I asked," I said, ignoring the reason he gave,
"Roxanne only just requested you join her and hers for a tete-a-tete
tomorrow afternoon. Something is going on. Don't ask me what.
Just something to shed lights. Some mystery-man to make explanations ... returned from wherever ... so you can kowtow and beg
forgiveness for not having seen the obvious all along. Stuff like that.
What do you think?"

"She does realize that if I suddenly turn up missing, that won't
stop shit from hitting the fan? All my thoughts have been written
down and, along with the Polaroids, are in the hands of someone
prepared to go public, with or without me."

"I would assume Roxanne assumes you are prepared to cover
your ass." Ass-u-me?

"I might be persuaded to drop my ass-cover for your hard cock."

"Jesus, Billing, don't you ever give up?"

"Nothing is ever gained by not putting out the effort." His smile
was seducively charming.

"Well, you might want to seriously rethink this cock-up-ass business, and ..."

"Your-cock-up-my-ass business, or vice versa?" he interrupted.

"... give it a rest," I finished off my thought. "In the meantime, check in with me tomorrow morning. Hopefully, by then, I'll have rendezvous specifics."

"Sure, why the hell not?" he shrugged, and ate more noodles. "Oh, by the way ..." The epitome of nonchalance, his preface for what was coming sounded harmless enough. "... you need to get yourself an airtight alibi for early evening, day after tomorrow."

"I beg your pardon?" Simultaneously, I tried to deal with a couple of particularly thick and rebellious sen yai.

"Something is going to be happening, at approximately eight P.M. It's best certain people be absolutely assured of your benign presence elsewhere at that time."

"Something happening? Certain people?" I said. "Could you be a tad more cryptic?"

"There's going to be a well-deserved execution," he said.

Which momentarily left me with a noodle half-in half-out my mouth, snake-like. "What in the hell do you mean, a well-deserved execution? Whose execution, for Christ's sake?"

He didn't answer.

My mind spun. Whose execution (click) would cause certain people (click) to question the validity (click) of my alibi (click) and have me on the list of suspects (click) who might have pulled the trigger, wielded the knife, or delivered whatever the hammer blow to leave someone's brains splattered on the wall (click, click, click)?

"Jesus!" I said. "You know who Madam Elephant is, don't you?"

No answer.

"Jeff?"

My calculating went into high gear: "You got to Kenneth Critzer before the police did."

I experienced a brief flash of that sprawled body, knife-punctured and dead in the park. Noodles, seconds before so delicious going down, went putrid in my belly. "You actually killed Critzer!" I hissed. "Jesus, you did. You did."

"I didn't say that," he said.

"Why not say it? Killing people is what you do, isn't it?"

"I never said that, either."

"Lt. Col. Chuab said it." Did he, though? If he hadn't said it, out and out, he'd certainly implied it, which was just the same.

"Don't believe everything the cops tell you," he said.

"Shouldn't you take pride in your profession?" I said. "You kill so well, why not brag about it? Critzer was even on the outlook for you. He said if he saw you, he'd bolt. He didn't bolt, though, did he? Probably he didn't even see you, you're so good. Jesus!" I put my head in my hands. "Jesus!"

"Don't get so excited, stud Stud. Whoever killed Critzer did humanity a favor. He was a sleaze. He supplied Madam Elephant with the gun that was supposed to blow us away on that riverbank. It was through no fault of his—in fact, it was a major inconvenience for him, that the weapon didn't work."

Suddenly, I knew why Jeff wouldn't come right out and say he'd done the deed. "You think I'm wired!"

"If I said, 'Yes,'" he said, "would you consent to a full body search?" If I ever wanted to see a sexually explicit sneer, this was it.

"Christ, Billing! Are we back to sex again? Does everything go back to that? Was it even a sex-thing with Critzer?"

"Come on, Stud, do give me credit for some taste."

"You killed him. I know you did."

"But that doesn't excite you, does it?"

"What do you mean, 'excite me'?" I was so dumbfounded, I had to repeat my response. "Are you fucking crazy?"

"I thought not," he said. "I can spot the types it does excite. And, make no mistake about it, they're out there. You might be surprised by how many of them there are, attracted to the dark side. Whatever, they're hot to experience bad stuff vicariously by bedding the bad guys and not getting their own hands dirty. But, since you're not one of them, does that mean that if I tell you, 'Sure, I've killed people, damn well killed Critzer, damn well am going to kill Madam Elephant,' that you'd suddenly lose that impressive boner in your pants? Or maybe you can't lose something that's such a permanent fixture. But do I have even less chance of getting to it? I think so."

"What in the fuck are you talking about?"

"I'm talking about your increased likelihood of going to bed with me as long as you're able to rationalize how I might not really be as bad as I'm painted, as long as you don't have proof I'm really that bad."

"Read my lips, Billing: I'm not going to bed with you! Ever!"

"Never is a long, long time."

"Fuck, why me? There's a world of gay guys, maybe even straights, who would jump at the chance to get in your pants, and I can't shake you off for love or money."

"Could it be because you're so goddamn sexy? Could it be because you're so goddamn handsome? Could it be because you play so goddamn hard to get, while too many gay guys, too many straight guys, are always too willing to climb into bed with me?"

I shook my head, at a loss as to what else to say.

"Have you never been bitten by the lust-bug, Stud? Have you never just suddenly seen somebody you wanted so damn badly that you felt your longing all of the way to the tip of each hair on your head? Knowing you could sneak up on him anytime, anywhere, he's so damn vulnerable!, and forcibly take him, except you know the taking would-n't, in the end, be what you wanted at all? What you want, what you've always wanted, is simply his, 'Yes, please.' And 'Thanks'."

"You fucking need professional help, Billing."

"I need a night in the sack with you, stud Stud."

"It's not going to happen."

"That just tells me that you've never experienced what real lust is all about. If you imagine yourself lucky to have lust's complica-tions out of your life, you've got it so wrong."

"Sex is not the be-all end-all," I said—this from someone who had spent a good many years fucking anything with a cunt and pre-tending that was the be-all end-all.

"That you're able to think that, let alone say it, confirms that you're the one, between us, who's the more fucked up. Because homo sapiens, even homosexual homo sapiens, are, by their very nature, sexual animals."

"Christ, what pyschobabble! Why don't I just refer you to my psychiatrist, so the two of you can go orgasmic discussing all of this bullshit while fucking each other?"

"About that offer you made of allowing me a full body search."

"Only in your dreams."

"I'll bet money Roxanne thinks she's going to get in your pants.

Are you going to let her?"

"None of your damned business."

"Do you know how few times in my life I've found myself actually verged on the brink of green-eyed jealousy?"

"Save me from hearing the numbers."

"Very few times—but in this case I dislike Roxanne for just that reason, as much as for her involvement in what's going down at the museum."

I was on the verge of putting definition to a vague suspicion in the back of my brain.

Madam: a woman. Elephant? The matriarchal hierarchy of pachyderm herds has been documented by a gamut of TV nature shows. All of the shit going down at the museum, Jeff's ongoing feud with Roxanne, insinuations of high-crime and misdemeanors. And let's not forget the less-than-honest dealings that had landed Powell Whyte his collection of Thai artifacts in the first place.

Could "bentness" sometimes be passed down in the genes from uncle to niece?

"Tell me it's not Roxanne, Jeff." I put the disconcerting possibility into words. There likely wasn't a more extended matriarchal industrial complex to be found, anywhere, than the one Roxanne headed.

"You better not know," Jeff said, "especially when your knowing will give you less convincing deniability when the time comes."

"Tell me it's not Roxanne, goddamn it!"

"It's not Roxanne, stud Stud."

"She's my friend, Jeff. She's my ... goddamn ... friend. Shit! I've known her since I was in school."

"Calm down, stud Stud."

"And how many times do I have to tell you to quit fucking calling me stud Stud!"

People stared; I didn't give a damn. Jeff scooted down and back in his chair. He crossed his arms in defensive posture.

"It's not Roxanne," he repeated. "It's not anyone you know. It'll just be a strange name when you hear it on the news or read it in the paper. It's merely important you recognize there will be people, after this man ... notice, I said 'man' ... this complete stranger to you ... is dead, who will remember he tried to have you killed, and who will think that you might well have responded with a counterattack.

Perhaps you identified him via bribes, or via your associations with low-lives like Sammy Ped Mai or Kenneth Critzer. Some people will care less that Madam Elephant is dead, but other people—displaced by the new crime-world pecking order—will likely be disgruntled, even vengeful. We—you and I—merely need to make sure your ass is covered. We wouldn't want anyone to get to it before me, would we?"

"Jesus, sex and murder in one breath."

"Hardly alpha-omega: no life's likely to result from our sex, except our liveliness beneath the sheets."

There were people for whom killing and death are aphrodisiac. Right now, it seemed quite probable to me that Jeff was one of those.

"How can you just kill someone? Even if, like Critzer, they are evil. How can you so calmly talk of killing someone else? Just like ..." I snapped my fingers. "... that!"

"Now, as regards your alibi." He was as tenacious as a pit bull. "I have some definite thoughts on the matter."

"Fuck your definite thoughts on the matter!"

He dropped his arms from his chest. He came forward over the tabletop. I pulled back as if he were a cobra about to strike.

"It's a done-deal, Stud. It's a going-to-happen thing. Nothing you can do is going to stop it. Nothing. Quit assuming the savior role and get your head out of your ass long enough to protect yourself from misdirected consequences."

"I don't believe this. I fucking ... do ... not ... believe."

"Believe!"

"What about your alibi?"

"I've arranged for one."

"One that, I'm sure, can eventually be seen through by anyone with enough bribe-money, or muscle."

"I'm good at dropping off the face of the earth. Who will give a rat's ass about who killed Madam Elephant in a year's time?"

Kenneth Critzer dead. Madam Elephant soon dead. Jeff their killer? Jeff gone! I couldn't separate my fear, my disappointment, my horror, my sadness, my ... my ... what?

"You're putting me into deeper therapy, you know that, don't you?"

He smiled. He thought I was kidding. (What would Dr. Melissa say if and when I called her on this one?)

"I want you to contact Sammy Ped Mai," Jeff said.

"You want me to contact Sammy," I said. "And, why in the hell would I want to contact Sammy? To tell him you're out to blow away the Supreme Deity in his fucked-up little world?"

"You want him to arrange a little show for you. It needn't even be private. In fact, he should feel free to have a few other interested, albeit discreet, voyeurs in attendance. Sammy, the businessman, will appreciate that you extend him the courtesy of better maximizing his profits."

I was speechless.

"Maybe for the performance, you should request someone you know. Say, this big-ram Ram guy."

Where and when had I ever said anything to Jeff ... of all people ... about Ram?

"Maybe you should ask for something you might actually find of interest, say a bit of B&D. Say, Ram in chains. I hear he's already volunteered, so all you have to do is check into schedule time and date."

Where in the hell did he get his information? But then, the walls of Texes Bob's off-the-disco maze aren't the thickest or most soundproof. How many pre-orgasmic grunts and orgasmic groans had I heard on my mere walk-through?

"I'd have the same iron-clad alibi if I stood in the middle of a busy Bangkok street and dared traffic to run over me," I said.

"My way is less dangerous—we don't want you run over—and it provides witnesses—Sammy Ped Mai, Ram—so much a part of Madam Elephant's world, it's far less conceivable they'd be persuaded to lie on your behalf than, say Roxanne."

I, too, came forward over the table. Our foreheads almost bumped. I smelled the pork broth from his noodles on his hot breath.

"Fucking ... fucking ... fucking madness!"

"Call Sammy today," he said. "It may take him time to set it up. Ram is extremely popular, the way I hear it. Although, I'm sure he'll extend the extra effort to rearrange his schedule to work you in."

He scooted back his chair. I grabbed for his forearm and missed. He saw my effort and waited.

"Tell me again it's not Roxanne," I said.

"It's not Roxanne," he said. "Trust me."

Trust him? Sweet Jesus!

He came forward again, close across the tabletop.

His arms reached across the place settings and the soup.

His arms retreated back across the table before I realized his intimate hands-on pat down for a wire was over and done. Curious restaurant patrons looked on equally amazed.

"What the fuck?" he said, his voice low, intimate, isolated entirely within the short space between us. "Why not tell you I've killed people for a living? I have. Why not tell you I killed Critzer? I did. The ignorant sonofabitch thought he was so clever but he didn't even see me coming. Why not confess that I'm going to kill Madam Elephant? I am, for all the reasons you can guess, and for all of the reasons your emotion-deprived brain can't guess. If my telling you all this keeps me from getting into your pants, who says you're even worth it, you screwed up little closet-queer fuck!"

Before I could answer, he left me trembling and covered with sweat.

10

Roxanne arrived at the house on Litchi Klong in time for lunch. She wore a rose-silk blouse and rose-silk slacks, with rose-silk bolero jacket. We ate chicken salad sandwiches and a mixed green salad with the Bel Di house dressing Roxanne shipped in regularly from the restaurant in Oregon State. She hadn't come, though, for the chicken salad sandwiches and salad.

"I'm afraid there will have to be another short delay in our meeting this afternoon with Billing and Mr. Tiller, " she apologized. "I'm only talking an hour, max."

"Mr. Tiller?"

"He's back in town but involved in the seizure of a crime organization warehouse." Which gave insinuation but not definition to his background. "You should make Billing understand that all of this is pertinent to the explanations he's after."

Jeff might well be made to understand. He might well have even expected the previous delay, the present delay, and additional delays, in Roxanne's ongoing efforts to put off answering his awkward questions.

I still kept faith that there were answers, however much it frustrated me that she refused to come up with them at every opportunity.

Perhaps sensing my frustration, she decided to toss me a bone.

"I suppose that shitty little pervert Sammy Ped Mai, turned up yesterday on your doorstep to boast how clever he is." Of course, she would have heard about it; I had no doubt Little Boy Blue on his motorcycle was still the talk of the neighborhood.

"Naturally, I didn't believe his version of events," I said. "Then I got to thinking, maybe you and I *did* make the trip north by car only so he or his men could more easily follow along."

"I really would have liked to put him in jail. His grandmother is convinced Sammy's gangland connections and his determination to get his hands on her recently acquired windfall, could get her more than just a black eye next time."

"In America, Sammy would have gotten off on a technicality called entrapment."

"Thailand isn't America," Roxanne said. Was she bragging, or complaining?

I didn't tell her a phone call from me had helped Sammy avoid her trap.

"So you did lie to me about that woman being Mrs. Trang." I was out to make her feel too guilty to see my guilt.

"After your meeting with Sammy in the hotel, it seemed possible he'd be in touch with you again. If you believed the woman we visited was Emily Trang, and Sammy believed you believed ..." She shrugged. "I couldn't trust you to come away from any meeting with him less than a bit charmed and ..."

"My God, 'charmed'?"

"Oh, he can be charming, my dear. Really, he can. And, when he's confronted with someone he finds prodigiously delicious ..."

"'Prodigiously delicious'?"

"His words, not mine."

"He certainly didn't say that to me."

So, did he say them to Damnern at the door yesterday?: "I'm here to see that prodigiously delicious Mr. Draqual. Will you tell him Sammy Ped Mai is here to see him, please?"

"So, who is the pseudo Nana with the tatting pillow?"

133

"Just someone who was willing to do a bit of acting for a fee."

"Are the tatting and the embroidery really hers?" If I could manage to get my hands on just a few more pieces ...

"I'm afraid they're not. Except for the green-dyed item, the whole collection belongs to a friend of mine. Which is why all the individual pieces are of such excellent quality. The collection was borrowed because everyone, including you, knew Emily Trang does that sort of thing. A good play must be performed with proper props and stage design."

"I'm not giving back my piece!"

"Of course you're not. It was an experiment in lace that I would likely have sold you, anyway. This way, we'll merely call it your fee for services rendered."

I would have preferred to continue our conversation while Roxanne was being so forthcoming, but she was called to the phone.

While she was away, I mimed enjoyment of my sandwich, my plate of greens, my serving of imported dressing, but my mind was racing.

Roxanne came back, but only to say, "I have to go. But we're still on with Billing for a little later."

"I can't guarantee Jeff will be happy by this latest delay." I didn't see why explanations for me required Jeff's presence. How would Roxanne deal with Jeff when I couldn't say for sure she wasn't playing him for a sucker?

Then, reading my thoughts, she reached out, stroked my hair, and said, "Stud, do please try to remember that all comes to those who wait. It's important for all involved that Billing do likewise."

That's what I told him, as soon as he'd climbed into the parked car at the prearranged pick-up point at the Kroa Road—Kotchasan Road intersection."

"Hey, Jeeves!" he greeted our driver; I hadn't even recognized the cop behind the wheel as the very same who had driven Jeff and me back to The Oriental after our interrogation. "Why am I not surprised the police are involved?"

Jeff settled back in the seat and looked damned good doing it, elevating his hips and providing an inadvertent bas-relief of his hard cock.

"So, what's the deal with this warehouse?" he wanted to know. "And why the delay?"

On cue, there was a blast of radio static from up front that our driver understood and answered, but which didn't give me a clue. I thought I caught a reference to "Status Blue".

"There's been gunfire at the take-down site," the driver said after he'd turned back over the seat in our direction. "We're to hold off on the rendezvous until further notice."

"What is it with Bangkok and gunfire?" I wanted to know.

A pedestrian, walking past the curb at which our car was parked looked in my direction, as if he'd heard my question.

"And, what is it with Bangkok and knife attacks, and attempted assassinations by dying in dyeing vats?" Jeff chimed in. "On the other hand, this latest exchange of bullets does gives us plenty of time to fuck up a storm right here in the backseat. Think the bouncing chassis will draw a crowd?"

"Jesus!" I said. I'd convinced myself that his tell-all at the noodle joint might have ended his sexual come-ons once and for all. I'd convinced myself they wouldn't be missed.

He smiled widely.

"Surely, you're not as surprised as you look?" he said. "You're smart enough to understand that getting you in bed without you knowing the real me wouldn't satisfy me. Actually, it took me a while to figure that out."

I shook my head.

"I had my first sexual experience in the backseat of a car. And you?"

"My business," I said.

"At your business, you say? Which of you was in the Draqualian-silk slip?"

"Funny." Not.

"Are you a virgin, stud?" He laughed. "Kind of an oxymoron, that! Virgin stud. Except, you do seem kind of virginal, which is actually rather charming."

"Ask me if I care."

"Do you care? Please, say yes. Pretty please."

"Or what? You throw a conniption?" I laughed. I couldn't help myself. The very notion, however passing, that I might end up, like Sammy Ped Mai, having people ask, "Please pass the Thesaurus," every time I opened my mouth, was something I found as funny as I found it scary.

"You should laugh more," Jeff said. "If you look really-really good, normally, you look really-really-really good when you laugh. I refer to your genuine laugh, though, and not to one of your usual half-ass sarcastic ha-ha's."

"Give me a break, Billing, huh?"

"How about I give you this?" One hand parenthesized the bulge of his already impressive basket.

"Jesus!" I said, saved from having to make any additional rebuff by another garbled radio communication.

"Code Green," the driver said, and we were in motion again.

Within minutes, we were waved through a roadblock and parked among all the other police vehicles.

"If anyone asks why you and I are arriving with hard-ons, what do we tell them?" Jeff asked.

I shifted a forearm to hide—from him and from Roxanne, the latter coming to my rescue by opening the back door—the visible effects of his renewed sexual banter.

"Stud," Roxanne nodded, then focused on Jeff. "Thank you for coming, Mr. Billing."

"I tried my best to come en route, but Stud wasn't having any of it," Jeff said.

"If you'll follow me, please," she said, ignoring his smutty humor. "The warehouse is finally ours even though its occupants were determined not to let us have it. We only learned of it because of some very intensive interrogation of one Mr. Mahn Sutohn."

My mind flashed on Mahn Sutohn, his pants down around his ankles, leaned up against a stolen bodhisattva, his asshole fucked by a camera-clicking Jeff.

"Ah!" said Jeff. "I assume you're talking about the same bastard who gave me access to the museum and then exposed me to all the resulting gunfire. Which leads me to suspect his revelations about the warehouse weren't voluntary."

"Until you told Stud, and Stud told us, that it was Mahn Sutohn who let you into the museum, we hadn't a clue of his criminal connections." Roxanne stepped back to let us out of the car, then led the way toward the industrial complex.

"The last of the warehouse security force was removed but minutes ago," Lt. Col. Chuab said, greeting us just inside the building. By the looks of his unruffled demeanor and wardrobe, the chore might have been less strenuous than a walk in the park. "Everyone from the other side headed for locales more conducive to successful questioning."

He motioned for us to follow him deeper into the dimly lit interior.

I was surprised and impressed by the sheer volume of the seized contraband.

"I see originals and forgeries, here," Jeff said.

"The originals have been pilfered from a whole range of Thai museums and archaeological sites," the Lt. Col. explained.

We passed a line of Buddhas, seated and standing, bronze and brass, porphyry and limestone; Devi and Siva statues and statuettes; headless, armless, and legless rock torsos; Ardhanari heads; votive plaques; sandstone figures of Uma, Vishnu, Hanuman, and Prajnaparamita.

"Through here is something of particular interest." Chuab steered our little party further through the labyrinth of metal and stone figures.

The preponderance of inanimate objects gave me the uneasy feeling I had somehow been made just another piece, and a minor one at that, in a complicated game of Oriental chess.

We stopped before two bodhisattvas, and a man joined us. His eyes were brown. His short-cropped hair was brown. His off-the-rack suit was brown. His oxfords were brown. His Caucasian skin was yellowish-brown from a poor sunlamp.

"Ah, Mr. Billing, isn't it?" he said; apparently I didn't merit mention. "Do you recognize what we have here?"

"Mr. Tiller, I presume," Jeff did his Stanley meeting Livingston routine. "With an accent that sounds British but not quite."

"An affectation picked up from long association with the Brits," Tiller said, sounding Yank but not quite.

"Officially employed by?" Jeff asked.

"Now? In the past? In the future? You know how it is." The latter wasn't a question.

"Your official title?"

"Persuader," Tiller obliged, but sounded uncertain. "Coaxer. Cajoler. Inveigler."

"Break someone's arm or a leg if he doesn't tell-er?"

Tiller's smile was patronizing, not in the least genuine, and punctuated by, "One of the good guys, at least in this instance, Mr. Billing."

"Called in by the Thai government," Roxanne said, running interference, "in order to personally supervise Mr. Sutohn's interrogation."

"These two bodhisattvas are the originals that are missing from the Powell Whyte Memorial Museum," Jeff finally answered Tiller's question.

"Yes," Tiller said, sounding like a computerized voice, slightly off-line.

"Two very valuable bodhisattvas, pre-Ankor style. And as anticipated by those in the know, both, along with the whole Whyte collection, a particularly juicy plum for organized crime's plucking. Every piece of the collection is of superior-grade, worth astronomical amounts to private dealers who can't hope to pick up anything comparable via legal channels in today's markets. The plan was to monitor the collection during its transfer and installation and to entrap the thieves in the act of theft or when they exchanged fakes for the originals."

"There were snags," Roxanne said. "Despite all of the monitoring, artifacts went missing. From a purely logistical standpoint, there had to be at least one bad guy working from inside the museum. We didn't know who that bad guy or guys might be, though, until Jeff inadvertently pointed a finger at Mahn Sutohn. As it turns out, Mr. Sutohn is merely the tip of the iceberg."

"You imply that the art thieves worked fully from within the museum hierarchy and could, despite all precautions, easily replace the original artifacts with fakes?" Jeff sounded doubtful.

"There are always ways for unscrupulous men to entice usually law-abiding citizens to silence or to cooperation, Mr. Billing," Lt. Col. Chuab said. "One way is the simple threat of murder. Another way is the threat of death for a loved one. A third way is the threat of unspeakable torture and mutilation. And of course there's always the fourth alternative of offering bribes."

A slight lift of Roxanne's hand was sufficient to shift everyone's attention back to her. "In an attempt to suck in the bad guys and identify them, we arranged for the appointments of Dr. Kan-buri and Dr. Rangliti as Thai art experts on the museum staff. Dr. Kan-buri has an expensive opium habit, and Dr. Rangliti is a ladies' man with a wife who'd rather have another cold piece of jewelry to keep her company on hot nights than her husband. Their habits made them vulnerable to an illicit approach. We could probably march Dr. Kan-buri and Dr. Rangliti through the museum at this very moment, and they'd swear the two fakes on site are the real things."

Time for my two-cents' worth. "There wasn't a word about the shooting at the museum in the media."

While Tiller and Chuab looked as if they'd prefer I imitate Lot's wife and turn into a statue of salt, Roxanne was more obliging. "We didn't want to draw attention that might compromise the operation. A public investigation of Billing having been shot might have inadvertently turned up the fakes. Questions would have been asked that might have proved embarrassing to the Thai government, which is officially in charge of museum security. I might have been asked, publicly, whether I considered I had grounds, under the default provisions of my uncle's will, to claim the collection for myself. All of which was unwanted publicity, in the face of the sting we were trying to accomplish."

"You complicated things, Billing." Tiller's accusation was begrudgingly complimentary, one professional to another.

"If my uncle stole all or part of his collection from the Thai people, he was prepared to make amends, albeit posthumously," Roxanne said. "I assure you, Mr. Billing, I have never been out to deny him his penance. I have more than enough money, without the collection, to last me my lifetime."

"Do you have any idea how many forgeries pass the inspection of supposed experts in reputable museums every year?" Tiller asked, addressing Jeff. "There's a kouros at the Getty Museum that some experts say is sixth-century B.C., but others swear it's twentieth-century A.D. There's a sarcophagus at the Boston Museum of Fine Arts that could be 45 B.C. or 1900 A.D.; it depends upon which expert is asked. There are yeas and nays for Raphael's 'La Fornarina' at the Barbierini Gallery in Rome. Is it any wonder that criminals are so confident that their replacements of original artworks with forgeries will go undetected in Thailand? If the experts can't always tell a bodhisattva, pre-Ankor style, from a bodhisattva, Khmer-style, do you expect doubts to be voiced by the ordinary man off the street? Certainly no one ever expected you to know the difference."

An eerily disembodied and urgent voice called out from somewhere deeper within the warehouse.

Tiller's turn toward the hail was automatic, graceful, precise. "Lt. Col. Chuab! It would seem we might have a ..."

The ear-deafening blast was succeeded by a chain reaction of fire, wind, and noise that roared through the complex toppling artwork and people like a Titan's dominoes.

The warehouse, as Lt. Col. Chuab bragged, may well have been ours, but as was later officially verified, the previous occupants hadn't left without a final statement—the series of staccato booby-trap bomb blasts that made the floor beneath me roll like Jell-O.

Unceremoniously, I lost my balance, collided with a wooden statue, and went down. A sunburst of white-hot light and hellish flame went off somewhere to my right.

Jeff stumbled away from me as shelves of surrounding pottery and standing Buddhas toppled in unison. By the time I got back on my feet, Jeff was lost in a ten-foot pile of burning rubble.

I hadn't a clue where Roxanne, Lt. Col. Chuab, or Tiller had gone. I only knew I was sucked into hell-fire and brimstone.

A resounding crack singled itself out from the general pandemonium. I turned toward it and saw a wooden platform in complete collapse. A large bronze statue of a demon spilled in my direction. I lifted my arms defensively, although I knew the statue would easily crush me. My palms flattened against incoming blast-heated bronze. I staggered beneath its weight and crumpled. I went down. My shoulders and head banged the floor. With an accompanying thud, the statue lodged just short of crushing me. I didn't ask why I'd been saved; I only took advantage. I squeezed out from under. The fallen demon's sword had bisected three fourths of a wooden Buddha before the blade had stuck a mere three feet short of the floor.

I was out of the frying pan but literally into the fire. Flames were all around me. Heat sucked sweat from my pores, moisture from my eyes, and toasted my skin. Combustion greedily stole my oxygen. Fire-roar drowned all other sounds. A metal Vishnu, perched atop the Garuna bird it so often rides in legend, glowed red in the furnace-like heat. A figure of chanda-li danced within a shower of sparks. A once highly polished Brahmin turned blackamoor beneath a fallout of greasy soot. It was a sea of flame whose navigable lanes were continually altered by falling statues and debris. I was forced to take whatever way presented itself. I stepped on and over the dented metal of a multi-armed Prajnaparamita and squeezed around the large stone head of a decapitated Dhammapala.

The whole world burned around me! What little breathing I managed became even more of a chore as billowing smoke grew thicker. I leaned exhausted against hot stone, part of a large seated Buddha that was mostly lost to the murk and the gloom. I turned head-on into a smoky breeze that reached me over a limestone Hari-Hara whose two left arms, one hand holding a seashell, lay broken at the figure's feet. I stumbled forward, past a terra-cotta deer whose folded legs gave it the collapsed appearance of a poor animal already succumbed to asphyxia.

Escape for me, if it existed, remained hidden within a river of smoke that grew thicker by the second. I surrendered to my remaining survival instincts, held my breath, and plunged forward. Desperately, I tried to see through the smoke, ash, and heat-distorted air. I wasn't sure how long I could hold my breath and keep going.

I instinctively knew it was Jeff who grabbed me: all hard muscle and confident control (like O'Reilly back in that New York alley, only Jeff hugged me from the front, O'Reilly had grabbed me from the rear). Jeff's chest was against my chest. Jeff's belly was against my belly. Jeff's hard cock battled my hard cock for whatever little space there was between us. Jeff's face was so close that his cheek pressed my cheek. He smelled of fire and brimstone, and fire and brimstone never smelled so good.

"I know the way out," he said. "Trust me."

"What about Roxanne?" I feared for her safety. I prayed for her life.

He didn't answer but danced us through the fire and flame like two gay guys in a ballroom, welded sensuously together. We literally waltzed—Jeff in the lead—through a frightening landscape made less so by the muscled arms that held me. Until finally, suddenly, the smoke lifted in a breath of fresh air, and we were outside. Behind us, the holocaust rose vertically, and its heat easily overpowered that of the Bangkok sun.

Jeff laughed his relief. His teeth were white against the tiger-stripe soot that blackened his face. I laughed, admittedly a tad more hysterically than Jeff did.

"How about that?" he said.

Though we still clung to one another, such contact quickly turned, at least for me, from needful to unacceptably intimate.

He hugged harder. His cheek and its slight stubble chafed my cheek. His crotch did a stripper's bumb-and-grind against mine. His lips were against my ear, actually—unbelievably!—nibbling while he panted loudly, and then . . .

Very quickly, he kissed me.

The room wasn't very large. The ten chairs weren't permanent fixtures, but were an eclectic arrangement of large wingbacks, bulky horse-hair, over-size leather, even fluffy chintz and Lazy-Boy recliner.

Only one chair was empty when I arrived. Unlike any other social occasion, eyes didn't turn in my direction. What kind of alibi would I have if no one paid me any mind?

I cleared my throat to get some attention. It didn't seem to work. My companions sat, with very little fidgeting, and looked pretty much straight ahead. Since the setting was theater-in-the-round, we all faced the elevated central circular platform that was the stage. The spaces between us left the possibility of conversation but didn't invite it. My seat was comfortable. It was some large super-soft, all-engulfing leather-upholstered nest that would have been equally at home in any den or men's smoker. Although sophisticated light fixtures dotted the ceiling, especially over the stage, the room was only dimly lit.

We became eleven with the addition of Sammy. His chair, decidedly small and dainty in comparison to ours, was carried in with Sammy already ensconced within it by a man so exceptionally well-muscled that he dwarfed Sammy and the diminutive chair even further.

Sammy played little boy dressed for first communion in a neat well-tailored white suit with an ivory rosebud in the lapel; a white shirt, white tie, and white Gucci loafers with tassels. His brief smile, though, was all priest-to-suppliants. He assumed the de rigueur straight-ahead posture, his back vertical, his hands folded demurely in his lap, his feet—somehow, despite the smallness of his chair— still not quite touching the floor.

The show announced itself not by a further dimming of lights, which would have plunged us into complete darkness, but by the appearance of a spot above the stage. The ignited column of bright- ness highlighted the lone post which, phallic and well-anchored, rose into the center of the beam.

A spot came on across the room, disclosing Ram. Half the audi- ence had to twist in their chairs to see him. He wore an intricate spider-web of leather that crisscrossed his body and exposed sexy and provocative glimpses of his bare skin. I looked for his trade- mark monster cock but couldn't see it. What I did see was the leather genital-pouch attached by snaps to three of the interwoven front-bands of his costume.

His progress to the stage was strobe-lit: a new light went on, the previous blinked off, as he progressed, one step at a time, between two chairs, to his final entrance onto the pole-centered stage.

This leather-clad apparition was distinctly different from the sexual robot of my Litchi Klong Road bedroom, and from the femme fatale of Sammy's office. Chameleon-like, Ram had shed all aspects of young-man prostitute and of sexy transvestite. He'd become All-Man personified. Even his musculature seemed to have obliged by having become more ropy and sinewy, no longer just skinny, svelte, or thin. Without saying anything, without doing any- thing but walk to the stage, stand there, and do his slow and easy look-at-me turn, he exuded palatable decadence and carnality. His black hair, this time his own, attractively tousled, banged his fore- head and feathered its tips among the inky strands of his eyebrows.

I was amazed and astounded by the three faces of Ram I'd seen so far. I wondered how many more existed and might yet be seen—by me.

He bent from his waist, and his hands went as far as the stage floor. His containing leather straps drooped seductively in places to reveal more tantalizing glimpses of his bare flesh. His skin was oiled—not to slippery greasiness but to a rich burnish. His small brown nipples enticed with their thumb tack erect centers. His navel was a small dome snuggled within a cupping crater.

"Mr. Draqual?" He had to say it twice before I realized he was addressing me.

He was still slightly bent. Chains, like macabre snakes, had materialized in his hands.

"What?" My one-word response was pregnant with self-consciousness. I was stared at now as an undeniable part of the show.

"Would you attach my leg manacles, please?"

Would I? I didn't know if I would or could. The couple of steps required seemed too great a distance for me to manage. Even if I could, did I want to? This newest personality of Ram—worldly, leather-clad, desirous of being chained for viewing pleasure—was alien, exciting, revolting.

Everyone waited.

Ram didn't repeat the invitation. He expected my compliance. My refusal was impossible. No cop-out was allowed. Everyone expected me, one more actor, to perform. Most everyone, with the possible exception of Sammy, was likely jealous that I was the one offered access to their ideal fantasy. I would be the one to kneel before him. I would be the one to touch his ankles and his iron manacles.

Sammy turned slightly in my direction, smiling.

As if disembodied, I floated those couple of steps to the stage, plus the step-up to stage-level; there to assume a subservient kneeling position and commence the attachment of the cool metal to his hot flesh. That Ram was the one chained, and I—who'd ordered it all up—was the one who knelt before him, to do his bidding, told the age-old B&D-S&M story in a nutshell. The anchored ends of the chains were firmly affixed to bolts within the stage slots from which they'd been withdrawn. The manacles clicked loudly and firmly into place. If they were magician's fetters, programmed to spring open at a touch, the secret of their key escaped me.

I sweated. Perspiration was steamy and soupy beneath my arms, at my crotch, and in a slow progression down the center of my chest.

"Now, my wrists to the pole, please. But first ..."

I'm still not sure where he got the gag that was a hard rubber ball with attached leather thongs. Maybe he'd walked in with it attached to some part of his costume. Maybe he'd had it in his hand from the start. From wherever he'd brought it to light, he handed it to me.

Even my simple recognition that he waited to be gagged, and I was the one supposed to do it, was hard-won. Ram's body heat was narcotic.

There were no, "For God's sake, hurry it up!" catcalls. There was no instruction. How much brainpower, after all, is required to put a hard rubber ball into a willing mouth and tie the thongs in place at the nape of a neck? How much intellect is needed to open cuffs around willing male wrists and squeeze metal shut? How many smarts are required to realize my procrastination provided its own, as yet acceptable, dynamic to the show in-progress?

Someone in the audience gasped orgasmically. I sensed shadowy hands kneading shadowy laps.

I was particularly careful in my descent. I was positive that, however careful, I would trip, sprawl, and nose-dive. I was reassured only in that my awaiting chair, extra-padded, was there to catch me. Sammy gave me a well-done, welcome-back nod. His air of knowledgeability was out of character with his accompanying Sunday-school boy caricature, and it contributed to the over-all perversity.

I sat and welcomed the all-encompassing embrace of my chair. I wiped sweat from my brow. My eyes blinked several times to dilute perspiration-sting. I re-focused on Ram. His well-choreographed struggles against the chains exquisitely mimed a trapped jungle cat vulnerability. I touched the bulge my cock made in the crotch of my pants. I told myself I did so to shift my dick's disconcerting stiffness to a more comfortable position, but once I had my hand against the ridge of my erection, it was hard to turn loose. It seemed as if my hand was as chained to my crotch as Ram was chained to the up-jut of the wooden post.

Ram's demeanor progressed to that of a captive beset by the reluctant realization, if not total acceptance, that the bonds holding him might be unbreakable. He was a prisoner who regrouped his thoughts and, possibly, revised his strategy. He was an actor who pensively considered the best odds for his escape from so undeniably abhorrent a situation. He eyed me over the lift of his arm and the curl of his snug-fitting iron bracelet. His taut body coaxed his pectorals and abdominals into an even more high-relief definition.

The distraction of an activated spotlight, again off-stage, almost wasn't enough to shift my attention from him. The newly appeared hooded leather-man was bigger than Ram. None of his hidden muscles needed to be persuaded into any farther exquisite definition, beneath the overlay of his tight long-sleeved leather body suit. The bump within his cod-piece was so sexily evident it appeared sheathed in form-molded elastic, rubber, Spandex, or techno-plastic wrap. The fully-clothed man was all the more sexy in contrast to his more naked victim. His clothing provided no immediate glimpse of his flesh beyond the surprisingly sexy peek of his tanned white-skin wrists where the terminals of his sleeves met up with his leather-gloved hands.

Only when he reached the stage and turned sideways did the bareness of his tattooed Caucasian ass first become evident, at least to me. His tattoo was of multi-colored rampant dragons, similar to the Draqual Coat of Arms, and it covered one of his wholly exposed and muscle-dimpled asscheeks.

Like a chained cat that spied the approaching dog, Ram tested his chains. He retreated as far as he could, in the face of the newcomer's blatant advances.

I expected a prolonged stalking. The suddenness of the launched attack, the jolt of immediately wrestling figures, one at such a decided disadvantage—flesh, leather, chains, sweat, heavy breathing—was made more dramatic by my incorrect estimation of timing.

In unison, several members of the audience, myself included, came forward in our seats. More than one cock shot through the forced openings of hastily breached flies. Stiff penile shafts were contained, held, wrestled, as Ram was contained, held, wrestled.

If not yet sexually united, attacker and victim had pretty much otherwise become one on stage. Ram's body was securely cupped from behind by the wrap of the other's muscled arms: muscled chest to victim's back, muscled belly to victim's butt, leather-sheathed cheek to victim's cheek.

The snaps that secured Ram's leather genital pouch were

released with such speed that it was difficult to see it happen. What was easier to see was how what was once concealed by leather suddenly sprouted, enormous, up and out from Ram's lower belly. His sac of heavy balls flopped audibly against his leather-banded thighs.

The audience gasped as one.

The hard and condom-rubberized cock of Ram's attacker was quickly brought to light by a skillful unveiling that dropped and hung the leather-man's codpiece like a miniature bib. The erection became all the more impressive as it jerked against the crisscross backdrop of leather that webbed Ram's exceedingly vulnerable ass.

The insertion of the leather-man's cock up Ram's ass was so speedily achieved even I recognized it as a flawed performance in need of better direction. While the surprise attack which had prefaced the actual fuck had turned into a kind of bonus, because of its pure unexpectedness, the actual placement of the cock up Ram's ass demanded far more finesse, a far more protracted lead-in, far more "sense of theater", than had been provided by this wham-bam-thrust-it-to-you-man.

Not that voyeuristic enjoyment was eliminated because of the frantic anal rape in progress. Sammy's hands alone remained unmoved and folded in his lap. My complaint was that of an aesthetic who detected "good" that could have been "great", if not for the selfishness of one man whom placed his satisfaction above the satisfaction of his audience.

Ram certainly couldn't be faulted for his part. His loud groans were of seemingly genuine agony.

I would have preferred that the attacker be out of his mask, at least by the commencement of the fuck. I wanted to judge for myself the degree of sexual ecstasy registered on his (handsome?) face, see if it was as convincing as the well-acted rape victim's rictus that twisted Ram's features. Maybe leather-man, some embassy minion or flight-crew attendant, wanted his identity kept secret, although his readily visible tattoo certainly might have I.D.'d him as surely as his face.

Ram's attacker likewise required more verbal skills. I fancied a spoken lead-in to orgasm. I fancied a step-by-step oration of the proceedings. I fancied a guttural grand finale. As it was, there was disappointingly little indication of actual orgasm. If orgasm was achieved. Except—maybe—the attacker's final grunt was a tad louder than those grunts that had preceded it. Except—maybe—an extra deep dimpling of the attacker's muscular butt cheeks that provided additional writhing of rampant dragons.

Proof positive of a successful leather-man ejaculation wasn't even evident after the swift withdrawal of his cock from Ram's anus. In fact, I actually expected him to attack again, maybe this time more slowly and with more audience-pleasing finesse. Instead, he briskly cut Ram's throat (my recollection of the knife, to this day, merely an unexpected flash within the ongoing columnar glare of the spot). Ram's body collapsed amid a cacophonous clank of death-weighted chains.

The corresponding quickness with which the killer made his exit, with no apparent hurry, made it seem as if Ram bled out on stage through some ill-conceived fault of his own.

The King and Queen of Thailand officially accepted, on behalf of the people of Thailand, from Roxanne Whyte, who represented her uncle's estate, the Powell White Memorial Collection of Thai artifacts to be housed in the newly dedicated Powell Whyte Memorial Museum. Roxanne's nasty burn and its bandage, evidence of her harrowing victory over the warehouse fire, were cleverly concealed by the diagonal-cut hemline of her exquisite black silk Perilli gown.

The King and Queen left the party early, but the crème de la crème of Thai society remained for more food, more drink, and more dancing. The reception was "the" occasion of that year's social calendar.

"Do you think Their Majesties hurried off because we Americans, and all Europeans present, would have expected them to gallop around the dance floor like the actors in *The King and I?*" Jeff asked.

He was handsome in his Guantarelle classic black tuxedo, ribbed white shirt, black-and-gold studs and cufflinks, black tie, black shoes. His arm was back in a sling. Had it been re-injured during the warehouse holocaust? I only knew his arm hadn't required any support immediately thereafter.

We stood on one of the museum balconies in hope of a bit of fresh air, though it was just about as muggy as the air we'd left inside.

"Well, *The King and I* has been banned in Thailand for a good many years," I said.

Jeff made me nervous, and not just because he stood too close on a balcony that had plenty of room to spare. My most recent dreams of him naked included his dimpled asscheek with a rampant-dragons tattoo.

"The rumor being circulated is that Ram was Madam Elephant," I said. Particularly disconcerting was how any truth in that rumor provided a motive for Jeff having followed through on his threats. "I saw Ram in drag, and he certainly looked like a real woman. No one can deny, either, that he was hung like an elephant."

"Is there a question in there somewhere?"

"If you dropped your pants, would I find dragons tattooed on one buttock?"

"No. But fake tattoos can be bought on any street corner. If I dropped my pants, you would find a real enough boner."

He scooted in closer and made me more nervous and sweaty. "What you really want to know is if I killed Ram a.k.a. Madam Elephant. Although you wouldn't be likely to forgive me had I used you to set him up, would you?"

"You said you would kill Madam Elephant that night."

He fished his inside tuxedo pocket and handed over the photograph of which I'd previously seen only a portion, the one Kenneth Critzer had been out to deliver when he'd ended up dead in a Bangkok park. Jeff's print contained the missing fourth person.

There was no question who the fourth person was. "Sammy Ped Mai is Madam Elephant?"

"Sammy wasn't supposed to be with you at Ram's performance," Jeff said. "I had it on good authority he'd be elsewhere. I was waiting, but he never showed."

Madam, then, was a purveyor of prostitution? Elephant, then, had something to do with the carved tusk on Sammy's office wall?

"This," I tapped the photo against the railing, "means you'll soon kill Sammy Ped Mai?"

"Sammy is safe enough for now. There's too much of a spotlight at the moment, what with the celebrity of Roxanne and your

involvement, the attempts to undermine the hand-over of the collection for underworld high-finance purposes, the booby-trapping
of the crime scene by retreating criminals, the death of the supposed
Madam Elephant, and all the rest. But, I'll admit I'm a patient man.
Look how long I've waited to get into your pants."

"One of Sammy's people may kill him before you ever do, you
know. Gangland's top-of-the-totem is always vulnerable to attack
from those lower down. Sammy isn't likely to have chocked up
many leadership points when he muffled exploiting the Powell
Whyte collection of Thai artifacts for profit."

"So we can agree that Sammy is destined for death one way or
another, then? That dispensed with, what say we shed what little
remains of the official pomp and circumstance and go back to my
hotel room for a lively romp in the sheets?"

"Oh, right!"

"Think about it," he said. "The timing and circumstances could-
n't be more perfect. We're two consenting adults. There's obviously
something cooking between us." I was still prepared to argue
against the latter, but he didn't give me the opportunity. "I'm again
disabled, due to a temporary setback..." He indicated his arm in its
sling. "... and thereby easy to control; no rolling you over in the
clover unless you want. I'm versatile enough, and confident enough
of my manhood, to provide whatever limited repertoire you may be
up to for the evening. Since I leave Bangkok first thing tomorrow
morning for parts unknown, there are no strings."

Of all the men who had ever propositioned me for sex, Jeff was
one of a kind. Not that his persistence was unique: some guys, gay
or straight, have egos that simply can't take no for an answer.
Maybe it was his playfulness of delivery, at least there on the balcony, that appealed to me. Just the way he said what he said had a
way of disarming me to anything other than the possibilities of fun
in bed with someone so dangerous but still with a sense of humor;
so manly but still with the ability to forgo the dominant sexual
role; so handsome but...

"Hey, you two!" Roxanne appeared at the entrance to the balcony. "What's a gal got to do to get a dance around here?"

"Sorry," Jeff said. "But I've got two left feet on the dance floor,
even without the additional encumbrance of this sling."

There were all sorts of excuses I could also have provided: a charley horse, an upset stomach, too much booze... "I'm game," I said. What was the purpose of a bolt hole provided by fate if I wasn't prepared to use it?

I offered Jeff the photo of Sammy Ped Mai and his international gangland cronies at Sangua la Grande.

"Keep it," he said. "Consider it a souvenir of our missed opportunity."

I pocketed the picture and took Roxanne to dance.

Jeff was gone the next morning.

"Mr. Billing has checked out," said the woman at The Oriental Hotel reception desk when I inquired.

There had been no reason for him to stay. So what made me think that despite what he'd said, he might stick around a few more days? Everything was neatly wrapped and tied, except ...

Lt. Col Chuab agreed to see me. The left sleeve of his neatly ironed uniform blouse was cut and hemmed to accommodate the dressing for a burn that extended from the bend of his elbow to include his thumb, index and fuck fingers. He frowned and shook his head when I asked if the police had a picture I could see of Rhee Dulouk. I'd never seen what the young Thai prostitute whose death had started it all looked like. Though Jeff had insisted Rhee hadn't really been his type, had merely been a warm body when one was needed, and then entertained Jeff with gossip about shenanigans at the museum—there must have been something about Rhee to make Jeff devote so much time and energy to finding the young prostitute's killer.

"You wouldn't want to see the crime photos," Lt. Col. Chuab said. "Even if I were authorized to show them to you, they aren't very pretty."

"Surely there must be one picture from before he was murdered."

"Your best bet for one of those would have been Rhee's boss, before the kid went independent."

"Sammy Ped Mai. No luck there."

"Actually Ko Ngan was his employer at the time. He ended up dead at about the same time as Rhee, although his murder wasn't nearly as well-publicized. His stable was taken over by one of his whores, Mary Racha. She owes me a favor. Whether she happens to have a photo of Rhee..." He shrugged.

He then invited me, as but one of a coterie of potentially interested VIPs, to attend the rescue of a second criminal cache of Thai forged and original artifacts. This sortie was geared specifically to put the authorities in a more favorable light than had their disastrous previous exercise at the warehouse. This time, it was promised, spoils which should go to the victor would go to the victor. They would not be allowed to be trashed by booby-trap incendiary bombs left behind by sore losers who preferred no one get the goodies if they couldn't have them. Having learned from their mistakes, the good guys, this time, had supposedly made every effort, before the fact, to see that any such explosives devices would be dismantled, not triggered by either a spoiled-sport enemy in retreat or by some inadvertent policeman.

This was being done in response to the general public, most of whom could no more tell a genuine artifact from a fake than me, but who kept hearing in the news how two very important pieces of the much-ballyhooed Powell Whyte Collection had gone up in flames in the botched raid. Lots of ordinary people were appalled by that wanton destruction of so many national treasures, which had been widely documented in video and print. Questions were being asked as to what kind of unpatriotic degenerates would so blatantly torch the nation's heritage, and what kind of unpatriotic police force had been too hamstrung to stop them?

Roxanne, who after all has all sorts of contacts, told me that the Thai Police had called in every favor owed any cop by each and every low-life on the street. Authorization had been given to use every available man, every available man-hour, every available bit of budget to locate this second major cache of stolen and forged artifacts so they could be safely rescued in toto from the bad guys.

"This Loi Kroa Road operation will be more choreographed than 'Swan Lake' by the Bolshoi," Roxanne laughed. She herself was begging off in favor of an appointment with her hair stylist; I, on the other hand, had nothing going that day before one o'clock.

"You had better believe that this time the police will have frisked every criminal present. The cops will have moles in place to overcome and subdue, disarm and deactivate. It's grandstanding, pure and simple. Not that I disapprove. It's important that the man on the street believes the authorities will always come out on top."

Of course that's not how it went. Someone ended up not exactly where he or she had been predicted to be, someone's gun ended up not where it was supposed to be, someone's reflexes were quicker than supposed to be. Gunshots were fired.

"Away from the parapet!" screamed the dapper lieutenant.

That's just where most of us were standing at the time. Viewers and cameras had moved en masse to that spot just as the helicopters dropped men to the top of the building directly across the street; cop cars pulled up screeching in front; flak-jacketed men raced up stairs, battered down doors; all amid a joyously loud din of sirens and shouts and splintering wood; helicopter rotors, and...

Did I mention the gunfire?

Many remained at the parapet even after the lieutenant's screamed warning. Because the problem with an orchestrated showboating of police acumen portrayed as a sort of press picnic in the park is that people might end up misconstruing real gunfire as celebratory pyrotechnics.

Not that I had to be told twice to get my ass out of the line of fire. After two experiences of being shot at (on a New York City street and in that Bangkok river taxi), I wasn't taking any chances.

"Damn it, away from the edge!" the lieutenant ordered all laggards. He looked far less a clone of his superior, Lt. Col. Chuab, now that his once shiny boots were scuffed by an uncoordinated stumble, and his uniform was soiled by an unintentional collision with a rooftop chimney.

The latest command wasn't backed up by the five other policemen on the rooftop who had dropped to cover. And since the short burst of gunfire had stopped almost as fast as it had begun, those who felt immune while it was going on felt invincible in its wake.

"That gunfire was probably nothing but special effects," Roxanne suggested later. "What's a police raid without a shoot-out? Give the viewers what they expect—some danger, some excitement."

Real bullets or no, it was pretty damned impressive when the bomb squad arrived. I unabashedly joined in the applause in appreciation of the sheer logistics involved, after the all-clear, in the successful manhandling of a hefty bronze Buddha into the street to be tipped face-down, nose sniffing the pavement.

Certainly, I was as interested as anyone by Lt. Col. Chuab's show-and-tell that included the new plastique explosive QNT (Quinitrotoluene), packed side by side with gel packets of naphthene plus palmitate, inside Exhibit Number One's hollow interior. I strained my neck, just as far and hard as the next guy, to see the indicated gyroscopic trigger mechanism that was motion sensitive. Also on show, trip wires so silk-thread thin that I had to take Chuab's word when he said he held one in his hand, and that it, and others, had threatened hellish swipes where they criss-crossed aisles like common cobwebs.

"All of this proves that these thieves might easily have destroyed these antiquities." Lt. Col. Chuab said.

I went directly from my meeting with Lt. Col. Chaub to my business lunch with Mr. Kamphang. For years Mr. Kamphang has tried to sell me silk f om his small silk-worm farm outside Renu Phanom. Each year, I must reluctantly tell him that the quality of his material, although it has improved, still doesn't meet the stringent standards of Draqual Fashions. Every year Mr. Kamphang smiles, nods his head in acceptance, and heads off to try again. I like his tenacity, and I'm as sure as he is that one of these years we'll sign a deal over our many cups of nam cha.

This year was no different. All too soon we exchanged our usual farewell handshake outside the restaurant, I saw him off in a tuk tuk and prepared to hail a ride for myself.

Someone's (or some thing's) sudden grab at my crotch came so close to manhandling the family jewels, I gave a reflexsive chopping hand movement that made contact with an audible thud.

I looked down on a young gamin who rubbed his suddenly welted forearm and eyed me with such an accusatory look of innocent beggar assaulted by ugly American that I immediately fished my pocket for some conciliatory spare change.

But, "The tampons are in the back of the store," he seemed to be saying, and waggled an envelope in my direction.

I really looked at him for the first time. Black hair with a humongous cowlick. Black eyes. Big ears. A horrible complexion. Skinny as a rail.

I assumed all of this was Jeff-related. Maybe Jeff was already involved in some new black ops gun-for-hire operation that required deep cover.

I took the envelope, the kid took my money and disappeared into the surrounding crowd, while two incoming tuk tuks collided in an effort to get to me. I walked over and leaned against the restaurant façade to take a better look at my prize. Inside the envelope was an ordinary three-by-five index card with the address of a building just a couple of blocks away written in a small neat script.

"Need a ride, American?" screamed an industrious tuk-tuk driver from the far side of the sidewalk.

I walked the distance instead and found myself standing in front of Garuna Mountaingear. Playing dumbfounded tourist, I asked the first friendly Thai face with which I could make eye contact (not all that easy in a polite society that tries to provide a person some privacy even on a busy Bangkok sidewalk), if I'd gotten my directions wrong. I was assured that I hadn't.

It was no more Jeff seated on the stool just inside the door than it had been inside that five-and-dime dress shop after my flight across the klong. This man had black hair, black eyes, a broken nose, clear complexion, and an impressively wiry physique. He flashed a fake wide smile that lasted only until I said: "I understand you have tampons for sale." I couldn't read his expression for shit, except it looked like its owner was someone who indulged an idiot.

He got up, pulled shut the front door, and turned a CLOSED sign toward the pedestrians and traffic outside. He inclined his head toward the rear.

I pushed through ropes of every shape and size that hung from the ceiling like dreadlocks. To be greeted by—ah, yes!—crampons. Far more indicative of Garuna Mountaingear than tampons, to be sure. The great thing about Bangkok is how it can provide anything anyone could ever want. But expecting crampons in the tropics is rather like expecting a woman mushing the Antarctic Ice Shelf to be wearing a string bikini.

Some of the crampons were genuinely antique. Most were rusted, with cleats too bent and dulled by neglect to provide safety on any ice floe.

A woman stood behind the counter, in the shadows. Her hair was concealed within a faded pink bandana. Her body was made nondescript by a faded pink sundress. All of that faded pink (reminiscent of sheets put too often through the washer) gave one very good clue, even before she said, "Hello, again, Mr. Draqual," in dulcimer tones.

"Miss ..." I had seen this woman stark naked and provocatively posed in a Sammy Ped Mai photograph, and she'd propositioned me for sex in my Litchi Klong bedroom, but I hadn't the faintest idea as to her name.

"Miss Nam Tan." Was there ever a more appropriate name for a prostitute than Miss "Sugar"? She moved into slightly better light. The only bulb was low watt. "Thank you for coming."

Had I known it wasn't Jeff at the end of the line, I wouldn't have bothered.

I didn't know if Miss Sugar's relationship with Ram had been purely business, but I told her I was sorry about how it had ended.

"So am I, Mr. Draqual, and not just because he was my brother."

Even if I did know siblings were simultaneously sold into lives of prostitution every day, having had two of them solicit me for menage-a-trois sex in the Litchi Klong house bedroom was more than a little shocking.

"Someone wrote a book," she said. "Some Italian, I think Ram said. Michelangelo?"

He was a painter and a sculptor. But did he ever write a book?

"Da Vinci?" I suggested. He was a painter. He wrote his notes backwards so they could only be read in a mirror.

Miss Sugar shook her head as if doing so might rearrange her brain cells into more cooperative alignment. The result was failure: I could tell by the way she bit her pouty lower lip and made it bleed.

"All about the changing of the guard," she said finally.

Jesus, she was confusing England with Italy, and what did anything Brit have to do with us, cooped up in this tiny space while I sweated a river and got claustrophobic in the bargain?

"People getting killed, as a matter of course, when the new replaces the old," she said.

"Ah, Machiavelli." I would have been more inclined toward Sun

Tzu if she hadn't specified Italian.

"You know him then?" As if Mac and I were on speaking terms.

If those closest to Ram were falling dead, as Miss Sugar insinuated, no one had likely been closer to him than his sister.

"I know things," she said.

I was sure she did, things likely as dangerous for her health as one thing had been for Kenneth Critzer.

"Lt. Col. Chuab can possibly help," I said but suddenly didn't believe it. I'd seen too many movies wherein the good guys promised, "We'll protect you," and the witness for the prosecution still turned up dead.

Miss Sugar found my token suggestion so ludicrous she dismissed it with a flick of her hand.

I wanted her to stop biting the same spot on her lower lip that was already bleeding and swollen. But I didn't say so.

"I know something you should know," she said; maybe it was time for me to mention Kenneth Critzer.

I was curious, sure. "For which I will, in turn, give you what?" I couldn't begin to imagine the last time or the circumstances under which Miss Sugar might have put out for free, other than per Sammy Ped Mai's instructions.

She produced a folded piece of paper from the pocket of her pink sundress, and slid it across the countertop toward me. Gingerly, as if it were a rattler poised to strike, I touched the edge and lifted along its fold.

It was a check made out to CASH.

"I have money," she said. "Lots. A large amount in a bank right here in Bangkok. Put there just for a time like this. Not to use but to sit as a distraction for certain people who would expect me to withdraw it for fleeing the city."

I wasn't sure of any possible health advantages from my being made privy to Miss Sugar's plans to leave Bangkok.

"I had cash put away for my real escape. Unfortunately a friend was made to disclose its location before I could get to it. Not the friend's fault, of course." She actually shuddered. Blood continued to ooze from the tooth puncture in her lip.

"And you want me to do what? Walk into your bank and cash your check for you?"

"I want you to be banker, give me my money now, but cash my check only after you're safely in New York City." Sure! Of course. Glad to agree. Yeah! "By the time you're back in Bangkok, I'll have been long forgotten. New will have replaced old for who knows how many more times."

Her predictions for the always quickly evolving criminal under-belly of the city at least sounded feasible. The real question was: what did Miss Sugar think she had to tell me that would get my cooperation?

"There's a branch of your Bangkok bank just around the cor-ner," she said.

I didn't ask how she knew that. I did pick her check up from the counter. "Perhaps, first, as a token of good faith, you might give me a little hint as to what you have for me?"

"Those booby-traps Lt. Col. Chuab keeps talking about on tele-vision," she said. "You need to avoid them."

Which provided me with enough incentive to pocket Miss Sugar's check, walk around the corner, and write a personal check of my own. After which I waited a short time that seemed like a very long time before the cash was counted out, put in an envelope, and handed over. Leaving me with the undeniable suspicion that I'd return to the mountain gear store and find both of the people I'd left there as dead as any Christmas goose.

But, the same guy unlocked the door and let me in, locking it behind me. Miss Sugar waited in the back room. She'd recognized what damage she'd done her lip and had put a Band-Aid on it.

I handed over the money.

Anxious to be rid of Bangkok or not, Miss Sugar counted every last baht. I felt like a john waiting with his pants down while a pros-titute dutifully took care of business.

"You have a knife," she said finally. "A blade so-so." She showed a six-inch space between her index fingers. "Triangular blade. Ivory handle." None of which was a question. But, then, hell, her brother had given it to me. "Get rid of it."

"Beg your pardon?"

"If you've shipped it to New York toss it as soon as you get home. If you've shown it to anyone, deny it. It's a disaster for you waiting to happen."

For Christ's sake, how much explosives could be packed into an ivory knife handle?!

Her turn to one side, breaking eye contact, told me she possibly thought she had given me my money's worth.

I reached across the counter, knocking crampons off with a force that caused one dull spike to scrape my forearm just before I clamped my fingers around Miss Sugar's wrist. If I regretted the obvious discomfort my squeezing was causing her (and I'm not at all sure I did), I might have ended up with more serious regrets if her bodyguard, who suddenly appeared at my side, had used the gun he aimed directly at me.

"No, Johnny!" Miss Sugar saved the day; I've never seen a charging bull pull up so damned fast as Johnny, and I've seen more than my share of corridas.

She asked him to go back up front, please, and (color him unwilling) he did.

Miss Sugar turned her full attention back to me and said, "You're fucking breaking my wrist!" It was only then, I realized I'd been shocked into gridlock. I turned loose. She would have one helluva nasty bruise.

"Tell me more about the knife," I said.

She sighed, rubbed her wrist, and looked genuinely put upon. So much emoting made me wonder if she'd be any better at faking an orgasm.

"Ram used the knife to kill Mr. Mullet and his companion," she said. An insinuation which, true or not, almost dropped me on the spot.

"Mullet?" She had made it rhyme with Hyacinth Bouquet. "Denny Mullet?" I didn't believe her. Not for a second. What in the hell kind of con game was she trying to pull? "He's spelunking for Christ's sake!"

Miss Nam Tan was confused. Evidenced by her quizzically pursed lips that bowed her Band-Aid like a caterpillar in mid-crawl. Simultaneously, her eyebrows scrunched, the bridge of her nose wrinkled, and she said, "Huh?"

"Caving," I elucidated. "Walking into a big hole in the ground."

"He's no longer walking, although probably still in that hole. Ram said he left the body in natural cold storage."

"Why in the hell would your brother kill Denny Mullet?"

She shook her head, not to insinuate she didn't know the answer; her expression labeled me a genuinely naïve and ignorant sonofabitch. "Mr. Mullet was after your lady, yes?"

"Ram killed Denny as some kind of perverted favor to me?"

Another shake of her head. Another get-real grimace. "You think it a favor to kill a man, leave his body somewhere cold enough so the cops can still identify one of a kind stab wounds, days maybe even months later, and leave you with the murder weapon?"

"What the fuck? I was hard-pressed to make any sense out of her madness.

She made the unlady-like sounds of raising phlem along her swan-slender throat. Seemed to consider where to spit, including on me. Swallowed.

"You made Ram hot and horny," she said. "Good news and bad news for you. He was out do everything he could to seduce you, but he hated wanting you so much."

I came at her again over the counter, just short of grabbing her neck.

"Why the fuck did your brother kill Denny Mullet?" I'd completely forgotten, at least temporarily, all references to Denny's friend having met a similar fate. "Why did Ram give me the murder weapon?"

"Who's going to pay any attention to someone spouting gibberish about a conspiracy at a museum when that someone is jailed for murdering his rival for the woman they both loved? A crime of passion is so much more juicy than any dry stuff about rusty artifacts."

"Christ, if your brother wanted to keep me from telling what he thought I knew, all he had to do was stick his knife in me at any time during the night we spent together."

"It would have been okay if you'd died at the river from sniper fire, because everyone thought those bullets were meant for Billing. But there would have been difficulty explaining you dead in the house on Litchi Klong Road. Too many questions would have been asked. You're high-profile. An American. Rich. A close friend of Ms. Whyte. You're less likely than Billing to have homicidal enemies. And don't even pretend to believe that everything crime bosses do doesn't come back to bite them on the ass. You want proof, take a look at how the booby-trapping of Thai artifacts turned the unwanted spotlight on so many people, my brother included."

She rubbed her wrist as if it were still sore. She rubbed her neck as if I'd grabbed hold and left fingerprints.

I would have asked her how I could possibly be accused of killing Denny when I was in Bangkok at the time he died. But I knew the answer from all the TV I'd watched in my lifetime. The longer the time before a body is discovered, the more difficult it is to pinpoint exact time of death. Killed between midnight and two, becomes sometime on Monday, becomes sometime within the last seventy-two hours, becomes sometime last week, last month, last year. By the time Ram got around to anonymously alerting the police to Denny's whereabouts, and the murder weapon still in my possession, there might have been all sorts of gaps in my Bangkok time-line. Though I certainly wasn't likely to forget my night with Ram, he could have conveniently forgotten. Providing the police with a suspicious window of opportunity during which I could easily have driven the couple of hours southeast to kill Denny and his friend (the potential witness), hidden their bodies, and returned to Bangkok. No one supposedly the wiser.

The bodies were still out there, and that was the thought I kept in the front of my mind as I left Miss Sugar and her bodyguard and hightailed it in a speedy motor-driven taxi to four-nine-six Litchi Klong Road. Where I had the taxi wait while I retrieved the murder weapon and the square of clean linen in which I'd wrapped it for safekeeping. I took the knife and the cab to the Oriental Pier. I rode one of the Express boats as far as the Chang Pier. And surreptitiously fed the knife to the ravenous river.

On the verge of my departure from Thailand, I met up with Sammy Ped Mai. Last time I'd seen him, he had seemed genuinely relieved Ram's killer had not turned out to be Sven Gaarlson, flight-attendant for Scandinavian Airlines, whom Sammy had officially booked for our little pseudo-rape party. Sven had been found after the murder, bound, gagged, and unconscious. Sammy's excuse for not recognizing the unauthorized substitution: "All westerners look alike to me." Followed by the less flippant: "Who knew? The guy was covered in leather, head to foot, except for a tattoo on his naked butt that he could have got inside any cereal-box."

This go-round, Sammy insisted I join him at his "little" house. The interior-interior room had been revamped from English drawing room to Arabian-Nights harem (Sammy's word for it: seraglio). Gauzy drapery was everywhere. An abundance of large throw cushions and rugs-over-rugs. A hookah in one corner. There was a camel saddle against one wall. A plethora of low furniture and lots of beaten brass.

"It's how I imagine Arabia, though unfortunately I've never been there," said Sammy.

He wore a red fez and a white blouse-shirt with puffy gusset sleeves. All six black frogs of his red vest were unfastened. Gossamer pale-blue pantaloons draped his legs, black slippers with red-tasseled, curled toes contained his feet. There was enough black kohl around his eyes to make him look downright raccoonish.

He sat perched on one of the cushions like a little-boy pasha. I sat cross-legged across from him on a prayer rug thrown atop a carpet that might well have been real Persian.

"You debarking soon?" Sammy said. He munched sugared dates from a convenient platter, and he offered me one, which I declined. "We shall miss you."

Again, he used the royal plural.

"You'll be back soon, we think, what with the silk business and all. You must be sure to call every time you pass through. We're always at your disposal. For favors done. You understand?"

I pulled the photo from my sports-coat jacket and laid it, face up and facing him, on the rug between us.

"Ah, yes," he said.

"That's you in the picture, isn't it?"

"Ah, yes. With three friends. Momentarily, I forget just where."

"The photo was taken on Sangua la Grande."

"Do you really think so?"

"These three men were certainly there," I said, and tapped the trio. "You, on the other hand ..." I shook my head.

"Undoubtedly, it is we," he said. "Admittedly, not our best likeness, but it is undeniably we, nonetheless."

"Your likeness, though, was inserted into this photograph via computer imagery," I said. "Anyway, that's what an expert tells me. What do you make of that?"

"We don't understand computers," Sammy said.

Maybe that was so. There hadn't been one visible in his office. I'd yet to spot one in his house.

"One only needs to know someone who knows computers to have such photo-magic done," I said. "Why is this a computer-generated Sammy? If Sammy Ped Mai wasn't in the original, who, if anyone, was?"

"So many questions!" He rolled his raccoon eyes. He ate another date and licked powdered sugar off of each finger as if it were a miniature cock.

"Why did Ram tell me you were once Rhee Dulouk's pimp, that you and Rhee quarreled, and that the jilted security guard from the museum had loud words with you, that Rhee left you?"

"Perhaps, we were Rhee's pimp. Perhaps, we did quarrel. Perhaps ..."

"... the moon is made of green cheese," I completed for him. "Ko Ngan was the purveyor in question. Probably the fight, if there ever was one, was between Rhee and him. Probably the loud words, if there were loud words, were between the jilted security guard and him. Probably he's the one Rhee left. Probably Ko Ngan was killed for the same reason Rhee was killed: secrets shared during pillow talk that hinted at crimeland money being made from the artifacts in the Powell Whyte Memorial Museum. Mary Racha took over Ko Ngan's business and she was able to give me this..."

I produced a second photo. It had been cropped by me, in that the original included Rhee Dulouk's medium-size cock, erect and fisted; his ass had been poised on the brink of descending onto a very large black dildo.

In the picture, Rhee Dulouk looked like a once perfect peach corrupted by over-ripeness. His eyes were still pretty and thick-lashed, but their look was old-age knowledgeable. His smile was still sweet and sensuous-lipped, but it lacked humor. His hair was still lush and stylishly razor-cut, but it had no gloss of youth.

"Jeff isn't likely to come back to Thailand to kill you, is he?" I said. "Madam Elephant is already dead in revenge for Rhee

163

Dulouk's murder. You set Madam Elephant up for murder. You saw that Ram was trussed up as securely as any sacrifical ram for the slaughter. Jeff carried out the assassination, fake tattoo, and all."

"Ram was a shit!" Sammy said between chews of another date; he wouldn't keep his boyish figure if he kept on eating like this. "He certainly was no friend to you. The only thing that saved you was that he saw how you could be used to help him set me up as patsy for Rhee's murder. Save his own neck from Billing who proved hard to kill and was deadly hot to kill whomever was responsible for ordering Rhee Dulouk dead. Ram wanted to kill two birds with one stone AND take over my business. That was his plan from Day One of his ascension to 'Madam-Elephant' crime-boss position."

Did I tell him about Ram's plan to have me blamed for Denny Mullet's murder? Nah! I wanted Sammy to do the talking.

"Ram wasn't content with pay-offs," Sammy obliged. "He wanted the whole goose that laid the golden eggs. His sexual pro-clivities put to good use by him when he came to 'work' for me, but really looking for a way to grab hold of my business from the inside out. He needed to be cunning, because I ..." Back to first-person sin-gular, was he? "... have my high-ranking friends. The game's not completely without its rules and regulations, you know?"

"Was it Ram, then, in the original photograph snapped in Sangua la Grande?"

"Only Kenneth Critzer is likely to have ever been persuaded to tell us that. He was so anxious to save his own skin, having sold Madam Elephant exploding guns. He would have sold his own mother into slavery for a reprieve. I only first saw the photo, with me in it, after Billing told me he had it. Billing far easier to find and to meet with than he was to be convinced by my, 'I think you are being set up to believe I am Madam Elephant.' He said, 'Oh, yeah, well I have a photo that proves otherwise.' Though I wasn't *really* in the photo, as you so cleverly discovered on your own. It was a struggle to persuade Billing to have the picture professionally ana-lyzed. Lucky, lucky for me he was persuaded. Unlucky, unlucky for Madam Elephant!"

"Please don't stop now," I encouraged.

"That Ram found you so physically attractive made it very easy to bait the trap. Ram was always too into sex to be a real leader.

Too ready, too willing, and too able, to mix business with pleasure. Another strike against him: the lucrative artifacts-for-cash project suddenly in shambles. That bit of ineptness made enemies of many of his original backers. It would only have been a matter of time before someone more clever and more qualified decided to move up the ladder. Bye-bye Ram! Bye-bye Madam Elephant! I just speeded the process, because I couldn't wait to see if someone killed him before he'd done away with me. Of course, I needed someone besides myself to do the actual deed because I live here, don't I? Don't want to soil my own nest, do I? Have to follow certain inherent guidelines, don't I? Honor among thieves, and all of that. No way I slit top-totem bastard's throat and get away with it."

Sammy Ped Mai's little-boy image was definitely gone. He looked every bit as old as he really was. However old that old really was.

Six months later, I was back in Bangkok to finalize the paperwork that would, for five years, provide Draqual Fashions with a continued monopoly on the Whyte Silk Consortium's output of the special green-dyed silk materials. The original two bolts I'd sent home, one tie-dyed, had been converted into Draqual originals that had proven to be runaway successes with our customers.

Denny Mullet and his friend were never found. When they hadn't returned from Panjumi Caves on schedule, there had been search parties. But the underground labyrinth is extensive, and wherever the dead men are stuffed remains a secret Ram took with him to the grave.

I'd completely lost track of Jeff. I sent out a few feelers to people I thought might know what had become of him, but nothing substantial ever came back.

Roxanne led the way up a minimalist stairway that was a helix of polished teak.

We were in her Bangkok condo. I was struck by how totally un-Thai it was. Strickette did NOT come to mind! Anyone shown a magazine layout of the place would be hard put to tell where in the world it exists.

She opened the door to the master bedroom.

We walked across plush egg-shell carpet to the open door of her walk-in closet. We strolled row after row of her hanging clothes.

Jeff had been a nomad when I'd met him. A nomad was what he'd remained. He'd only stayed in Thailand as long as he had to resolve and revenge the murder of an ex-trick who had turned up bloody and dying, one morning, on his doorstep.

Roxanne selected a vintage Yves St. Laurent pantsuit. She picked a blouse by Mikaratu Manshumattamorji, a Japanese designer whose name I never pronounce correctly but which always rolls, like honey, off Roxanne's tongue.

Back in the bedroom proper, Roxanne worked the blouse hanger to a mating with the other. She spread the result on her bedspread.

"Come on, Stud, the tie!"

I undid the green tie-dyed silk tie from beneath the stiff collar of my dress shirt.

She folded my tie in on itself and tucked the result up, and in, against the buttoned high neckline of her blouse on the bed. "There! Didn't I tell you I had just the outfit for it?"

Had Jeff truly believed my knowledge that he'd used me as a Judas' goat to sucker Ram for slaughter would keep me out of his bed? When he knew I wouldn't go to bed with him on any account, hadn't he as much as told me he was the killer when he presented me with the doctored photo? Had Roxanne's arrival on the museum balcony halted any verbal confession he might have been prepared to give me?

"The tie is yours," I said graciously. The completion of our recent business dealings left me genuinely magnanimous. She'd driven a hard bargain, but we both knew she could have come out even better.

With an all-inclusive sweep of one arm, she emptied the bed of all materials except bedding. My penis operated on the same automatic pilot it always did. The thumb of my left hand hooked the left front pocket of my trousers. My fingers angled downward to better accentuate the boner in my pants. We got undressed.

I've never, except in my dreams, seen Jeff naked. Unless, of course, I accept the possibility that it was his bare butt, muscled and firm, hard and dimpled, parenthesized by leather, fucking the protesting Ram.

Roxanne and I went to bed. We did a bit of simple cuddling. We did a bit of simple entwining-of-limbs. We did a bit of simple skin-against-skin. We did a bit of simple, "Hmmmm, you do feel so good!"

In my dreams, Jeff's body is always studly perfection: a Greek ideal come to life, sculptured marble metamorphosed into warm and silky and tanned and sensuous flesh stretched over a superb anatomical infrastructure.

I joined Roxanne in some mutual exploratory petting. My light-fingered touches wandered here, there, everywhere. Hers were butterfly wings that just barely grazed in passing.

Her nipples and mine were hard, getting harder.

In my dreams, Jeff's nipples are golden and dime-size, his pectorals square. There's a thin veneer of fine brown hair that fans the top of his chest but concentrates, straight-line, within the deep groove of his pectoral cleavage, for a vertical bisection of his chest and mid-section as far as his shallow innie navel.

My hands wandered Roxanne's belly. They skirted her cunt as if it wasn't there.

In my dreams, Jeff's abdominals are scalloped, his pubic hair curly.

I kissed Roxanne's forehead. I kissed the bridge of her nose. I kissed her chin. I kissed the arc of her neck. I kissed her breasts. I kissed her navel. Gently, my lips brushed through her pubic bush. I was well aware of just how much the upthrust of her hips invited my face to touch down.

Instead, I concentrated on Roxanne's below-cunt body. There was so much, even there, baby, that could do such nice things for me. There were her thighs... her knees... her feet ... her toes. All so incredibly sexy, including her burn scar which meandered her left ankle and calf.

Anyway, that's the illusion I hopefully presented.

"God, how lovely!" I said.

I pushed open her legs and kissed the spots that supposedly so pleased me.

When I raised my head slightly, did I see, without a touch to verify, signs of wetness gathered at the already slightly distended doorway of her pussy? Did the vertical slit of her cunt move slightly, as come-hither shiny as any lipstick-glossed mouth in need of a kiss?

In my dreams, Jeff's erect cock is thick and circumcised. Its head is vividly pink, its mouth slightly wet. His asshole is a small kiss-like pucker damp with sweat and lost—but easily found—between the press of his buttcheeks and the exquisite crack of his ass.

Roxanne groaned when I kissed her instep. Purred as my kisses rained on her knees, thighs, belly, and tits. Her whole body arched slightly when I kissed the jugular notch at the base of her throat.

Ever so lightly, I nibbled my way back down her body to her cunt. Not for a deep-sea muff-dive. It was merely a gentle touchdown made airy by my face rested atop the bush of her pubic hair. My tongue quickly flicked, but I avoided contact with her clit which was swollen and ("Ohhhhhh!") tender.

It helped that I like Roxanne. It helped that we are friends. How much did it help? Unfortunately, it wasn't the keystone, I'm sure, that it should have been.

"Here," I said, my face against her cheek, my breath recently freshened by peppermint.

How, I wondered even now, had Jeff's leather-clad cheek felt against Ram's naked cheek? How had Jeff's hot and ragged gasps for breath smelled in that sex-charged showroom?

Roxanne's hand caressed my flank to my ass, slid around to my belly and touched down along my cock.

In my dreams, Jeff's finger stops at the head of my erection.

"Look how hot you make me," I said, and it wasn't a lie.

I lay back and let one of her surprisingly rough palms thoroughly explore my dick. Merely by touch, she undoubtedly discerned the difference between love-wand and battering-ram. Was she disappointed that my cock might not prove big enough to provide any bonus of pleasure above and beyond the spurts of life-giving sperm we both knew she was really after?

Her hand went to my ass, her fingers dipping just a bit into the sweatiness of the crease. My hand went to her cunt, one finger gently dipping into the moisture.

And if it had been Jeff's rough hand fondling my ass, my fingers gently petting his erection?

My first fingertip-to-clit contact, and she groaned.

Is Jeff a groaner?

Some men find lengthy lead-ins hard to accomplish. Their libidos kick in. Their control centers shift from their heads to their groins. Their sexual drives whip them into virtual frenzies. Or, so I've heard.

Is Jeff one of those men?

Loss of control never happens to me. However, should I fuck a woman more than once... sometimes as quickly as screw two... she may sense something missing. Perhaps she thinks it's lack of spontaneity. One woman, cajoled and pressed to put a definition to screw three, put my dick and me, on the pleasure scale, somewhere slightly north of a battery-powered dildo.

What spurred me to make my first fuck of Roxanne genuinely memorable for her was my sense that she wasn't where she was— on the bed with me, naked—because of the pleasure she thought I could or couldn't give her. Since she wanted my sperm, pure and simple, she wouldn't likely have complained had I supplied it by a simple jump in her saddle and a ride to quick and selfish climax.

Jeff would have wanted—demanded—so much more.

I opted to further prime Roxanne's cunt and gave it my tongue before I gave it my erection. So many men are unwilling to go down there. It's as if down there is somehow too tainted by cock to provide suitable dining. It's as if eating cunt is cock-sucking by proxy.

What is it like to suck—Jeff's—dick? What would it be like to have him suck mine?

I licked my way back up Roxanne's body. "I want to kiss you."

I offered her whatever aphrodisiacal residue her cunt had left on my lips.

Why can't I remember how Jeff's lips felt, pressed against mine at the warehouse fire? Nor recall their touch when I was unconscious from the blast at the hotel?

When Roxanne gave a bit of tongue, I gave a bit of mine in return. When she bit my lower lip, I bit her upper lip. For awhile, whatever she did, I responded in kind.

My fingertips verified new moisture leaking to her same honeypot surfaces I'd so recently sucked dry.

"Can I fuck you?" I asked. I wasn't a thief come to steal favors in the dead night.

"Yes," she said. "Fuck me. Jesus, fill me!"

"Do you want to put my cock in for me?" I asked. No denying, I wanted her to do just that.

And she did touch my cock. And she did maneuver it closer to where we both wanted it to go.

What would be the difference if it were Jeff's fist directing my prick toward funkier confines?

My hands went flat to the bed, on each side of her shoulders, I arched my torso, up and back, my arms straight and extended. Roxanne was able to look down between her splayed breasts and see what she held and where she could put it.

"For just a moment... your cockhead... rubbing... the opening of my sweet pussy?" she suggested.

And she knew exactly where to drag my cockhead up and back... where to whip it left and right... where to rest its swollen tip.

"Yesssss," she hissed.

"Yesssss," I echoed, as equally at the boiling point as she was.

Slowly, easily, one sweet inserted-cock-inch at a time, I paid particular attention to her clit, which had gone bead-like. I varied my angle of entry. Her clit was like an old-time phonograph needle that I could make groove, hard or lightly, or not at all, down the length of my entering erection.

My pubic hair mingled with hers.

My cock slid to its final depth.

I paused in additional assurance I wasn't going anywhere, even at this point, without her say-so. In later fucks, this point would be a dead giveaway, in that what normal man remains quite so calm and cool, even disassociated, at the completion of so luxurious a slide of his hard and primed cock up moist and vise-gripping pussy?

"Fuck me," she said.

I began to do just that... slow and easy... in and out... easy and slow... out and in. Simultaneously, I smoothed her hair out of her eyes.

Jeff's hair is such a deep and luxurious mink-brown!

I ran a finger along the bridge of Roxanne's nose. I kissed the tip of her nose. I let her know her cunt still wasn't the only part of her that I loved, even at this stage of the game.

How fast I fucked her depended upon how fast she ask me, and she knew just what momentum she preferred. "Faster!"—"Slower!"— "Just a bit slower!"—"Just a bit faster!"—"Jesus, faster!"

My trigger mechanism never has anything to do with friction, along and back, the length of my dick. Always, it has to do with something inside of me that's strangely out-of-sync mental. Whereby, I merely say to myself, "Okay, it's time to end all of this bullshit. Let's get it over and done. Let's do what's expected." At which point, if my scrotum hasn't already lost all of its flaccidness, hasn't yet jerked itself up tightly to the base of my still-fucking dick, it does so. After which, it's only a matter of a few short seconds.

A thoroughly unexpected and disconcerting "something" occurred near fuck's end. So incongruous was my sudden mind's-eye image of me riding Jeff Billing's hard and naked ass that I was taken completely off-guard by the sudden upsurge of pleasure.

"Dear Jesus!" Roxanne said. She bounced her sweaty and seemingly out-of-control finale beneath me.

For a moment, I lost all sense of reality. When I could speak, I said hoarsely, "I do think that was my best fuck ever."

"Tell me about it, stud Stud," she said.

END